BILLY SUNDOWN

Billy Sundown, a Cheyenne Indian, was determined to return the young English woman to her home, so he took her from the blood bath that was the battle of Washita. But Billy, white educated, albeit with an Indian's temperament, was up against more than a tough trek to north Texas. In Pine Bluffs he was forced to kill two men and some-where on his back-trail there was a Pinkerton man. Meanwhile, on his ranch, John Grey had sworn to take bloody revenge on the Indians who had kidnapped his daughter . . .

*Books by Jack Sheriff
in the Linford Western Library:*

BURY HIM DEEP, IN TOMBSTONE

THE MAN FROM THE
    STAKED PLAINS

INCIDENT AT POWDER RIVER

BLACK DAY AT HANGDOG

KID KANTRELL

STARLIGHT

JACK SHERIFF

BILLY SUNDOWN

Complete and Unabridged

LINFORD
Leicester

First published in Great Britain in 2002 by
Robert Hale Limited
London

First Linford Edition
published 2004
by arrangement with
Robert Hale Limited
London

British Library CIP Data

Sheriff, Jack
  Billy Sundown.—Large print ed.—
  Linford western library
  1. Large type books
  2. Western stories
  I. Title
  823.9′14 [F]

  ISBN 1–84395–170–3

Published by
F. A. Thorpe (Publishing)
Anstey, Leicestershire

Set by Words & Graphics Ltd.
Anstey, Leicestershire
Printed and bound in Great Britain by
T. J. International Ltd., Padstow, Cornwall

This book is printed on acid-free paper

PART ONE

ESCAPE

1

Indian Territory,
Friday, 27 November 1868.
An icy breeze sloughed across the pines, brushing the powdery snow from the high branches so that it drifted down in the darkness to settle like gossamer on his face. Yet still he lay motionless under the heavy buffalo robes, blinking away the melting flakes, ignoring the knife-sharp pain in his eyes from long minutes of peering into the night.

The rustling of the breeze had disturbed the English girl. Thirty yards away across the clearing she tensed, then faded silently into the trees still some twenty yards from the picketed horses, and a flicker of amusement stirred within him.

The short rawhide cord that had tethered her to his ankle lay like a snake curling through a patch of snow-covered grass that shone in the pale moonlight alongside the glowing embers of the smokeless fire he had built when he had decided that they were safe from pursuit.

On the other side of the buffalo robes where she had lain sleepless the cord's end was ragged. He guessed she had worked on it with a sharp rock that had quickly grown slippery with her own blood, and again marvelled at how she had cut through the tough rawhide without disturbing his sleep.

The breeze died. The girl resumed her stealthy movements, a ghostly shape drifting out of the trees, the moonlight gleaming on the pale skin of one naked shoulder. She picked her way barefoot through the snow, with patience and infinite care. Each painful step took her closer to the dozing ponies, and he guessed that under the tattered cotton dress her heart would be pounding, her breath tight in her throat — and suddenly the amusement he had felt

4

was swamped by a surge of pity.

The small pinto sensed her approach. It lifted its head and snorted softly. She stiffened. As she turned her face quickly to look back across the clearing, her wide eyes glowed yellow in the dim light like those of an animal. Even across the clearing he heard her soft intake of breath, could almost smell her terror.

But when she turned away, reached out a hand towards the pinto, he knew that she had gone far enough and he slid smoothly from under the robe and came up on all fours.

He balanced on toes and fingertips, then sprang cat-like to his feet and launched himself across the clearing. The snow hissed at his passing. She sensed his approach and turned with a shrill squeal of fright and stumbled back against the pony.

He reached her in ten long, raking strides. The pinto jerked up its head and whinnied, tried to back off, snapped the picket line taut. Then he had folded the girl in his muscular embrace, clamping her arms to her sides as she fought like a wildcat. Head thrown back she writhed in his grasp, eyes wild and staring. Her knee came up hard against his deer-skin hip-leggings, aimed viciously for the softness of his groin. He slipped the thrust with ease, took the blow on the hard muscle of his thigh, turned his face aside as she spat her hatred. Like a snake she wriggled one arm free, moaned in frustration as she hammered futilely at his naked chest, the porcupine quills around his neck rattling under the blows.

'There's no need for this,' he said quietly, as the fury spent its force against the iron of his muscles and she went limp, her skin slippery in his grasp. 'I bind you for your own safety; everything I do is for a reason, you must trust me.'

'Then let me go,' she gasped. 'Turn me loose — '

'When the time is right.'

'Now is right.'

'No.'

'Then you're a liar.' She glared at him in the moonlight, her jaw thrusting with contempt, two angry spots of colour in her pale cheeks. 'Not only a liar, but a fool. You are a Cheyenne in a land that that is being taken by the white men, and you have taken an English woman as your captive. When they find you, you will hang.'

'Then for your sake,' he said gravely, 'you must hope that these savage men do not find me; for when they have finished with me they will look at you afresh, and soon hanging will seem like an easy way out.'

2

Billy Sundown forced the pace, riding in a north-westerly direction and always keeping on the fringe of high timber where the shadows were deep and he could ride with just one side exposed, and vulnerable. Always vigilant, he saw in the mud or expanses of patchy snow no tracks but their own, or those of deer or coyote; saw no movement but the drift of clouds and the swaying of tall trees in the cutting wind.

In such a manner he had, by nightfall on the eighth day, left behind the Washita and the Cheyenne reservation, splashed through a ford to cross the icy waters of the North Canadian and, in the warmer air away from the high altitudes, the tired ponies were pricking their ears as they scented the waters of Wolf Creek.

On the pinto, the young English-woman was huddled in a buffalo robe, riding with her head bowed, her long hair a dark veil across her face. She had long since ceased her frantic struggling, but Sundown knew that there was wet blood from the reopened wounds on her wrists caused by her steady, persistent straining against the rawhide thongs. The last time he had offered her water she had stared at him from hollow eyes feverish with hate. He had expected her to spit the liquid in his face, but at the first touch of moistness on her dry lips she had pushed her face against the cold, distended water-bag and swallowed without thought, her stubborn inflexibility betrayed by her raging thirst.

The moonlight glistened on the water. Somewhere, a long way back towards the high country of the Wichita Mountains, a coyote barked. The riders rounded a wooded spur and began the descent of a long, easy slope. Ten minutes later, at the edge of a stand of cottonwoods on the banks of Wolf Creek, Sundown slid from his horse. He gazed west, to where the night skies were faintly splashed with yellow light, and nodded his satisfaction.

'You know where we are?'

She was rigid in his arms when he enfolded the bundle of fur and helped her down from the pinto. Though muscle-sore and weary beyond thought, her head was held high.

'Tell me,' she said, her voice hoarse. 'Show me how clever you are.'

'This is Wolf Creek.' He waited, saw no flicker of understanding in her eyes. 'Thirty miles north of here it flows into the North Canadian. Five miles west there's a town called Pine Bluffs.'

She shook her head angrily. 'You're wasting your time. Of the whole of this hated country, I know my father's ranch and the area close by. This could be anywhere.'

'But it's not.' He looked at her pensively, thought of telling her more but knew it would be wrong. To do

10

what it was necessary for him to do in Pine Bluffs, he must leave her. It was best that, when he left, she remained in ignorance.

He led her deep into the chill, damp cottonwoods. In a small clearing where the darkness was less intense he sat her down on the trunk of a fallen tree, then swiftly brought in the horses and tethered the pinto. Then he lit a small, smokeless fire, gathered dead leaves and brush and scattered them to form a bed on the cold earth. On that makeshift bed he spread the warm buffalo robe that he had used to keep the cold off his own naked shoulders.

When he went to her, carrying the coiled length of rawhide, he saw the pain in her eyes and his resolve softened.

'I will be gone for some time, maybe most of the night.' He saw the flare of hope in her swift glance, and went on doggedly, 'When I leave you now I will leave you bound and gagged, close enough to the fire for warmth, but not so close that you can use it to gain freedom. If you need some thoughts to sustain you, I can give you this much: I told you that when the time is right, you would be freed; that time is very close. For more than three days I have been telling you I am taking you home. I tell you again: when I set you free, it will be within the gates of your father's ranch.'

'I don't believe you. I've fought you this far because I know that for some reason, you're lying. I'll keep fighting until I drop.' She laughed, her soft lips twisted in a grimace of disdain. 'In any case, if you were that foolish my father would shoot you down like a dog.'

'Foolish?' He tilted his head, puzzled by the thought that what this girl desired most was to be returned to her home, yet when he told her he would do that, he was not honourable, not brave — but foolish!

He clamped his jaw and dragged her from the log, forced into brutality by his need for haste and the sudden ferocity of her struggles. Feeling his quick temper rise at her obstinacy, he threw her down on the buffalo robes, gagged her with strips of cloth torn from the tattered dress, then secured the length of rawhide from the thongs fastening her wrists to the bole of a nearby tree.

When he rode out of the woods her muffled grunts of anguish and outrage went with him. Then he dismissed them from his mind. The winds of the winter night were like shards of ice cutting into his naked skin as he flattened his body along the horse's flowing mane and urged it into a gallop that carried him swiftly towards the nearby town.

★　★　★

Snatched from his tribe in a bloody raid by renegade whites when a youth of twelve, the young Indian called Awakening had later watched every one of the outlaws gunned down by a posse, then been taken by those hard-bitten

13

men to a harsh school run by devout Quakers where he was forced to learn the white man's language and customs. The Quakers were strict but always fair and, in their way, kindly, but there were frequent visitors who considered Indian children no better than the mangy dogs they kept tied up in the dust outside their own crumbling soddies. One man, with bleak eyes and prematurely grey hair and a temperament like a powder keg alongside a hot stove, had always picked out Awakening for the hardest kicks, and it was his face above all others that the young Indian tucked away at the back of his mind.

Despite the knocks, Awakening had remained there not because of the Quaker's vigilance or the locks on the solid doors, but out of choice: in his first twelve years he had learned about the land from experience, and of his own people, from his own people; now he was looking at that knowledge from a different angle, and studied avidly.

Over the next five years he had

benefited from the white man's education system, and come to understand that the Indians' only sin was that they were occupying rich lands coveted by the white man; they were standing in the way of progress and expansion. When he had learned sufficient, he left, and on his return to his people and his tribe he had taken with him the knowledge that progress was inevitable, and that the old ways were dying.

The boy of seventeen had been welcomed with grave satisfaction by those who remembered him, and his old name returned with him. But the eagle-eyed tribal elders had looked at him closely, had perhaps in their wisdom seen within him disturbing changes of which the boy himself was unaware and, with a suggestion of deep foreboding, they gave him a new name that, in rough translation, emerged as Billy Sundown.

By the time they reached the Washita, Sundown was twenty years old, and a man.

★ ★ ★

Camped on the Washita, the Cheyenne chief, Black Kettle, had been aware that one of their captives was from the Texas ranch of a man called Grey. When Billy Sundown set eyes on Jemima Grey, he was stunned by her beauty, and by the fierce defiance in the girl's blue eyes in the face of taunts and savage beatings by the squaws. But he also felt an ache in his heart that was totally unexpected. Each day her presence reminded him uncomfortably of his own years of exile, but his decision to take her and return the girl to her home had not been made until Custer's 7th Cavalry ripped brutally into the peaceful Indian encampment.

They came in out of a frozen, misty dawn, their horses crunching across the snow as they bore down on the birch-bark lodges with the smoke of cooking fires curling from their conical peaks. A rifle cracked. A brass band, incongruous and utterly out of place, burst into the 'Garry Owen', and raucous bugles sounded the *Charge*.

Sundown was one of the first out. He saw other naked braves leaping from their tepees and bounding with rifles and bows and arrows to take cover in snow-choked gullies as blood spattered the trampled snow and the air was filled with the squealing of horses and squaws and the stink of cordite. He saw Black Kettle go down alongside his wife, watched in horror as Sub-chief Little-Rock died defending his family, and children were trampled under the slashing hooves. And he turned away, sickened, and knew what he must do.

Once the decision was made, Sundown knew that it had been inevitable, and that for him there could be no going back. If the old ways were dying, a man had the choice of dying with them, or moving on. Though he could not deny his heritage, his years of exile had shown him that the white man's ways, like the ways of the Indian, were a mixture of bad and good.

In the midst of that carnage, the terrified screams, the crackle of rifle and pistol fire, the shrill bugle calls and the squeals of excited horses trampling the blood-spattered snow as they wheeled and turned in the cold mist that was like coiled smoke drifting in off the Washita, it had been easy for Sundown to find the girl, but not so easy to slip away.

The sight of the cavalry had excited her, and her instant reaction had been to burst from the tepee where she was being held and show herself to the charging cavalry.

She had not given a single rational thought to the cold-eyed, bloodthirsty squaws efficiently going about their cruel work, or to her own danger.

Even as he warded off the swinging rifle of a whooping cavalryman and sprang towards her, Sundown saw a young white boy disembowelled by the slashing blade of a cold-faced woman who left him dying in the snow and turned to seek out other white victims.

And as a horrified Jemima Grey stared wide-eyed and clapped a hand to her mouth and half a dozen squaws caught sight of her and howled their rage, a volley of erratic gunfire sent a hail of bullets ripping through the village. Sundown grasped the white woman around the waist and threw her bodily back inside the tepee.

The hail of hot lead offered respite. He let the tepee flap drop, saw the furious squaws cowering in the snow to avoid the bullets while their hate-filled black eyes watched Sundown.

Thirty seconds later, Sundown's own blade had slit open the rear of the tepee and he had unceremoniously slung Jemima Grey across his shoulder and was running with her towards the horses.

During the first day's desperate flight into the hills, Sundown had realized that the only way he could ride into the Circle G with the girl and stay alive was to go in as a white man — but his features made that difficult. The purpose of the journey to the Panhandle town of Pine Bluffs was to steal clothes, and saddles for the horses. That would go some way to creating the right image. The rest he hadn't worked out, but his placid, fatalistic nature was telling him to let events unfold, then adapt the situation to meet his needs.

The oil lamps of Pine Bluffs appeared as haloed pin-pricks of yellow light through the cold night air. As he drew nearer, Sundown called up memories of towns he had known, then cut across the end of main street at an angle and circled around the cluster of false-fronted buildings to ride in through an unlit alley. Amid the myriad unfamiliar smells he at once detected the scent of horse ordure, and straw, caught the soft sounds of horses blowing and, with a click of satisfaction, he wheeled the horse and brought it in at the back of the livery stable.

The doors were open, back and front. When he slipped inside and looked up the runway he could see clear through to Pine Bluff's main street. Yellow light from the town's oil-lamps flooded in. Two men rode past, slouched in the saddle, heading out of town. Across the street a cigarette glowed in the shadows, and there was the murmur of conversation. The sound of rough male laughter carried thinly on the night air. A piano tinkled. A woman began to sing, off-key.

Shutting his ears to the sounds, Billy Sundown cast a swift glance around the interior of the barn. At the top end of the runway, close to the street, a lamp glowed in the window of a small office. The door was closed, and Sundown guessed the hostler was in there, dozing. Horses moved restlessly in the stalls, aware of his presence, their hooves rustling the straw. Saddles were draped over rails. Sundown padded across, ran his hands over the supple, shiny leather, nodded in the gloom.

Then, quite close by and drawing

nearer, spurs tinkled and footsteps thudded on the plankwalk; irregularly spaced, unevenly weighted, as if the man making them was lurching unsteadily from side to side.

Like a shadow moving within deeper shadows, Billy Sundown slipped up the line of stalls and went around their end to stand in the pool of darkness alongside the wide doorway opposite the office. Across the street, the cigarette still glowed. From this close he could now see the outline of two men lounging up against the building, the sweep of their Stetsons, the glint of watching eyes.

Then the drunk came around the edge of the doorway, a man dressed in black, wearing a flat-crowned hat decorated with silver conchos, with jingling Mexican spurs buckled to black boots and a fancy six-gun in a tied-down holster.

The right size, Sundown noted. Medium height, and slim. His own size . . .

With the speed of a striking rattlesnake, Billy Sundown reached out and hooked an arm round the man's neck. His other hand came up and clamped over the loose, wet mouth. The man snorted through his nostrils, kicked out. An elbow drove back, ramming against the ridges of hard muscle protecting Sundown's belly. Sundown leant back, thrust with his hip and lifted the man clear of the ground. Silently, he swung him out of the light spilling in from the street and into the shadows. Porcupine quills rattled. The man heard the sound, was suddenly aware of oiled skin, the naked forearm clamped across his throat. He began a desperate, panicked grunting. Sundown tightened his grip, his knotted forearm like an iron bar across the man's soft throat. The grunts were choked off, became a sobbing wheeze. Swiftly, Sundown removed his hand from the man's mouth, placed his forearm behind the greasy head and pushed. There was a muffled crack.

The head went strangely loose. The man went limp, became a dead weight in Sundown's grip.

The office door clicked, swung open.

'What the hell's goin' on?'

Holding the dead man upright, Sundown became as unmoving as the old timber walls.

The hostler stepped out of the office, a small, old man, scratching a tangled mop of grey hair. Heat from a glowing pot-bellied stove wafted out with him, carrying with it the sharp aroma of strong coffee. He peered down the runway, hoisted his red galluses up over bony shoulders, then turned to the street and called out to the men lounging in the shadows.

'Jake? You see anything funny goin' on?'

A cigarette arced, bounced sparking, then hissed out in the wet mud. 'Nah! Ramon went in after his horse, that's all.'

'I don't see him.'

'Your eyes're angled too high.' The

man called Jake chuckled. 'That fast-shootin' 'breed's so drunk he won't be on his horse, he'll be underneath lookin' up at its belly.'

'I reckon that's where he kin stay,' the hostler grumbled. 'He may be lightnin' fast with that fancy pistol, but that don't give him the right to wake a man up without no danged reason.'

Still grumbling, he went back into the office and slammed the door.

As a tin cup clattered against a coffee-pot behind the closed door, Billy Sundown let his held breath go, then lowered the dead 'breed to the ground and quickly stripped him of his clothes. He removed his own breech cloth, hip-leggings and elk-skin moccasins, donned the 'breed's clothes and boots, slipped his knife inside the right boot and buckled the man's gunbelt about his waist. He bent, picked up the man's hat. As he did so, a silver concho came loose and fell to the runway, tinkling.

The nearby scuff of boots brought him swinging around. When he turned, standing so that he was shielding the naked body from sight, the two men from across the street were walking in through the double doors, one of them laughing nastily as they headed for the office.

A horse snorted as Sundown slipped the knife from his boot and moved like a ghost along the wall towards the nearest stall. But he was accustomed to soft moccasins, not high-heeled boots. He stumbled. The Mexican spurs tinkled. Both men turned without haste, caught sight of the black-clad figure in the shadows. Their faces split into wide grins.

'You was wrong, Jake,' one man commented. 'That Ramon, he sure can hold his liquor.' He moved away from his companion and started across the runway. Jake stayed where he was, still grinning. Again the office door swung open. The hostler was outlined against the lamplight, a tin cup in his hand.

'For Gawd's sake, Quent, get him on his horse and out of here,' he growled.

'Hell!' Quent said, startled. His eyes had flicked sideways, picked out the pale shape lying in the shadows. They darted back to Sundown, saw the raven hair brushing the wide shoulders. 'Jake, that ain't Ramon!'

In a flash, his right hand dropped to his six-gun, plucked it out of oiled leather. But Sundown was already moving. He took two bounding strides, brought his right hand up in a twisting, looping blow and slammed his fist, clamped around the knife's hilt, against the hard bone behind the man's ear — once, and again. The man grunted and went down in a crumpled heap, the six-gun spinning away through the loose straw.

Jake's pistol was out. He cocked it with a metallic snap. As his eyes widened and he lifted the six-gun level there was a whisper of sound. Sundown's arm moved like the lash of a whip. From a distance of ten feet the knife flickered through the air. The gleaming blade took Jake in the hollow at the base of his throat, sank in to the hilt. He staggered back, choking wetly, slammed against the office and slid down, his shirt-front already wet with blood.

Sundown followed the knife. He leaped over the sprawled body, reached the office as the hostler's tin cup clattered to the floor, liquid slopping. The old man reached behind him, fumbled in the rack by the door for a shotgun. Then Sundown was on him. He pulled the unfamiliar six-gun, cocked it, rammed the muzzle up into the folds of flesh under the hostler's chin.

'Still,' he said softly. 'Very still.'

The shotgun clunked to the boards. The hostler's rheumy eyes glittered.

'Damn Injun,' he spat. 'Git it over with.'

'All I want is two saddles,' Sundown said. He put away the pistol, gripped the old man's arm with fingers like steel, pulled him out of the office and held him still while he removed the knife from Jake's neck and wiped the blood on the dead man's shirt. Then, slipping the knife into his boot, he moved with the hostler down the runway. 'Jake and Ramon have no more need for mounts, or rigs. Get those saddles and bridles, put the best on my pony.'

'Goddamn red varmint!'

Held at the point of Sundown's pistol and spitting a non-stop stream of curses, the old hostler completed the task. Five minutes later he was back, locked in the office, and the lights were fading behind Sundown as he rode out of Pine Bluffs atop a fancy, centre-fired A-fork saddle, with an old McClellan braced across his thighs.

But before he left the hostler to yell his lungs out in the locked room, Sundown had stowed his own discarded Indian garments in his saddle-bags, then taken a quick sweep around the cluttered office and come up with a clean cotton shirt and pants and a plaid mackinaw that boasted all its buttons.

All three, he reckoned, would fit Jemima Grey where they touched.

★ ★ ★

She was sitting on the dead tree, the buffalo robe about her shoulders. The firelight flickered on her face, throwing shifting, upward shadows and glinting in her eyes so that against the backdrop of dark woods she lost the appearance of a young woman and became a sinister figure, filled with menace.

'It's the only way,' Sundown said softly, from across the fire. 'I have the white man's clothes, his fancy saddle and boots, the pistol — but with long hair, to your father I will still be an Indian.'

'And you'll trust me with this sharp knife? Trust me to stand behind you?'

The broad blade of the knife he had handed to her glittered as she held it up, turning it so that pin-points of reflected firelight touched Sundown's high cheekbones, shone on the drooping forelock and the long black hair brushing the shoulders of the 'breed gunslinger's shirt he had stolen.

'I trust you.'

She nodded, her eyes unreadable. 'Do you? But even so, somehow you'll manage to hold your new pistol on me, cocked, so that if the knife should slip, we both die.'

'Here,' he said sharply, and he drew the 'breed's .44 and reached out to place it on the wet ground between his feet in their tooled leather boots.

'That means nothing . . . you're stronger than me . . . ' She shrugged helplessly.

He smiled as she stood up, the menace slipping away with the eerie shadows as she circled the fire, now a forlorn figure in shirt and pants and the baggy mackinaw.

'There's another reason for this,' Sundown said. 'When you're finished, we'll talk . . . '

She slipped through the fire's pungent smoke and moved behind him, her feet in the Indian sandals rustling through the dead leaves. He felt her fingertips like the sharp points of icicles on his neck, the sudden painful tightening of his scalp as she roughly gathered his loose hair, twisted it in her hand and pulled it towards her. Then she stopped. He could hear her breathing, shallow, too fast; the faint tremor in the hand gripping his hair.

Suddenly the soft warmth of her belly was pressed tight against his shoulders. She hooked her other arm, bringing the knife around so that the back of its broad blade was under his chin. The grip on his hair became fierce, pulling back and down, lifting his chin.

For an instant, as the knife slipped down so that the cool metal was smooth against his throat, so that — as she turned it — he felt the hot bite of the razor-sharp edge, he thought he had lost. Then she gasped, as if in release. The knife was withdrawn, moved around behind his neck, and she began hacking at his hair. She worked fast, almost in a frenzy, wrenching at his scalp, slashing at the greased locks. When she had finished the night air was cool on his neck. She tossed the knife down by the fire. Her hands touched his shoulders and, as if she were about to collapse, her weight pressed down on him.

Sundown reached up to grasp her wrists, pulled her around in front of him. She sank to her knees, drained to the point of exhaustion. As her eyes flew to the thin thread of blood on his throat, Sundown said gravely, 'Now, you see? We are together in this. It is not the one thing, nor the other, it is both things together. Without me, you would have been taken by the squaws. Without you . . . ' He paused, reached behind him to touch the ragged edges of his hair, and she watched him, her eyes huge.

'Now do you trust me?' Sundown asked.

'Why are you doing this? Why did you slip away from your people? All right, the squaws would have . . . ' She swallowed. 'The squaws would have killed me,' she said, 'but why should that be your concern?'

'You don't listen — '

'I listen, but I don't understand!'

'Then listen with your eyes,' Sundown said, and he looked at the white girl, let his eyes caress the soft contours of her face glistening damp in the flickering light of the fire, let them move to take in the slender shape of her, graceful still even though wilting, exhausted, kneeling in dead leaves; lifted them to meet the sudden awakening in her gaze. 'Listen with your eyes,' he said again, 'and with your senses, and then tell me, Jemima Grey: do you trust me?'

The cold breeze lifted the trees and sent tendrils of smoke writhing and, as the smoke touched her and was caught in the loose cascade of her hair, she swallowed, rocked back on her heels.

'I've known you closely for just a few days. At the Washita I saw you often, and . . . '

He waited.

'And you were different. I knew that.'

And still he waited, with the patience of his kind, as she reached down to the damp leaves with her hand and with the tips of her fingers absently moved them and found the dark and glossy mass that was his crudely shorn hair; then realized, and touched it again but now with intent and, as she allowed the dark hair to slip slowly through her fingers, her eyes lifted to meet his.

And again, for a third time, he said, 'Do you trust me?'

'I trust you,' she said huskily.

He lifted his hands, placed his palms on her cold cheeks, bent forward to kiss her cold forehead.

'I trust you,' she said again, then shook her head numbly. 'But I don't trust my father. You're taking me home — and I'm frightened for you, Sundown.'

3

Tall, as lean as a fence post, and with a deceptively mild expression on his face as he stood on the gallery and gazed unseeing into the cold haze hanging over the sprawling plains to the north-west, John Grey was an Englishman whose unquenchable spirit of adventure had always brought him trouble.

In an attempt to settle down after bloody action in several small wars around the globe this stubborn man, who was like spring steel inside a velvet glove, had made money in dealings on the London Stock Exchange, turned that capital into a small fortune through his involvement with the termination of the East India Company's power on the sub-continent and gone on to marry a debutante who had provided him with a beautiful daughter.

But even twenty years of the very different kind of excitement that came from making money and acquiring enviable status could not forever stifle his restless spirit. One day, brutally and without warning, he told the women of his family that he was giving up his life in London and setting sail for America. He would risk his entire fortune in an attempt to raise cattle in the untamed wilderness that was the American West.

His wife had haughtily turned her back on him. His daughter, blue eyes dancing, had clung to him and expressed her support. They had sailed within the month, John Grey had acquired land in the young state of Texas within six, and he and his daughter were settled within the year.

And now this.

Somewhere out there, Jemima was in the hands of a savage. Grey's jaw muscles bunched at the thought. His steel-blue eyes narrowed in genuine pain, for the vision he had before him was far worse than any physical torture.

Somewhere out there . . .

And it seemed that nobody was prepared to do a damn thing to help, nobody was willing or able to ride out into the territories to locate and rescue —

Footsteps thumped solidly on the gallery steps, breaking into his thoughts, and Grey mentally shook himself and turned to face his foreman.

'Well?'

Ford Maddock, medium height, black hair raggedly cut and burned the colour of old saddle-leather by the sun, slapped his hat against his pants, gazed with amusement at the cloud of dust that drifted towards Grey, and shrugged.

'Jeb Horn figures you're gettin' hot under the collar over nothing. A couple of fancy steers missing — '

'Pedigree breeding bulls!'

'His words. I introduced myself, told him of your troubles. He's a mite contemptuous of those who figure they're a cut above the rest.'

'Are those his words, too — or yours?' A Circle G hand for just a few days, the new foreman came across to Grey as a man with strong opinions but with a suggestion of weakness in his character, and he was still being tested.

Maddock shrugged, let the question ride. 'He's also of the opinion you'd still have those pedigree bulls if you'd kept them penned instead of putting a fence around the whole damn spread and lettin' them roam.'

'I'd still have those pedigree bulls,' Grey said tightly, 'if Deacon Wood hadn't pulled down half a mile of fence in the dead of night and allowed them to stray.'

'His cattle need water, he's forced to use the ox-bow.'

'If he comes here and talks, I'll listen.'

'That's not his way. This has always been open range. A fence is an irritation. And now he's got more trouble.'

'Such as?'

'He had a couple of men killed up in Pine Bluffs, the day I was there chasing up that special feed.'

'Rumour?'

'Fact. There was talk in the saloon about a fracas in the livery barn.'

'Tough, but that doesn't alter the fact that he has my bulls.' Grey came away from the rail, dipped into his shirt pocket for a thin cigar, struck a match on his boot-sole and blew a stream of blue smoke. 'That's theft, rustling, whatever the hell you call it out here — and Marshal Jeb Horn has a duty to perform.'

'On any ordinary day of the year he's got so much to do he feels like he's hog-tied,' Maddock said, a grin twitching his lips. 'Most of those jobs seem a mite more important than negotiating the release of a couple of four-legged hostages.'

Grey frowned, flicked ash from the cigar, walked to the front rail and looked out over the yard. He sensed his foreman waiting for a response, but felt lost for words. He was well aware that his prize Aberdeen Anguses were not in any danger, and had quickly reached the conclusion that Deacon Wood was using them like an expensive pistol pointed at his head to force him to remove all his fences.

But, despite Maddock's words, these were not ordinary days, and one pressing problem tended to influence a man's thinking so that everything else became irrelevant. The bulls were safe, but the same could not be said for Jemima. She had been taken by savages on the open range Wood was so proud of, and transported to Indian Territory. Gut reaction screamed that she was priority, and that the men who took her should be pursued by the forces of the law — such as they were. But common sense told Grey that Jeb Horn was one ordinary man responsible for a small Texas county, and answerable to the sheriff; even if he was willing to put himself out, his hands were tied.

Amost inaudibly Grey said, 'Fine,

he's a busy man with rules to abide by, I understand that — but I'd like to believe he was putting some effort into finding my daughter.'

Behind him, Maddock said, 'I mentioned your concern. Horn did point out that a Pinkerton man's been sent into the Nations.'

'I know. And I know how long he's been out there.'

Maddock swore softly. 'Goddamnit, what is it you want? Countless white folk go missing. You think every one of them can be traced?'

Grey turned, stood stiffly against the rail. 'I think a reasonable effort can be made, and one third-rate detective chasing his tail hardly qualifies.'

'Neither of those terms apply to Jim Fleet.'

'For God's sake, the man's a professional investigator, born and brought up in the West! Why is he dragging his heels? He *must* know where she is, where she's been taken.'

'That was common knowledge from

the day your girl rode out on that fancy thoroughbred and went missing.'

'Then why, in almost two weeks, has Fleet failed to deliver? The Cheyenne are primitive savages, easily outwitted by a civilized man with brains.' Grey laughed. 'Or am I giving Fleet credit for something he doesn't possess?'

'What you're doing,' Maddock said patiently, 'is making a big mistake by not giving enough credit to the Cheyenne. Not only are they clever, in their own society those redskins are civilized — '

'Civilized!' Grey swung around, his face flushed. 'Damnit, man, they took white hostages, held them against their will — tortured them brutally!'

'They're fighting, in the only way they know how, to hold on to the land they've made their home.'

'What the hell makes it their land?'

'I didn't say that,' Maddock said mildly. 'It's not their land, and they acknowledge that fact in their religion and their traditions. But they occupy

43

it — and if that doesn't give them some claim to it after God knows how many thousand years, it surely doesn't make it the white man's.'

With a savage gesture Grey hurled the cigar from him and turned back to the rail, his fists clenched as the big foreman moved to the top of the steps.

'Leave it to Fleet,' Maddock advised, stepping down into the yard. 'He could do nothing when your girl was held captive in Black Kettle's village. Now she's out and running, he stands a chance.'

'Really?' Grey shot a glance at the foreman. 'The rumour is that Jemima's been moved from Black Kettle's encampment on the banks of the Washita. She's now in the hands of a lone savage.'

'Hard facts are that George Custer stormed that camp in the dawn light and gunned down Black Kettle and a host of others — so you might do some thinking and ask yourself why that savage took her.'

'I have,' Grey spat. 'There's only one answer I can come up with, and it sickens me.'

'What if you're wrong? What if he's done you a favour?'

'And what's that supposed to mean? Are you telling me it's easier for Fleet to find her?'

'What I'm saying,' Maddock said, 'is that Indian must have his reasons. And, yes, all right, when Fleet does locate her, with one Indian to come up against he'll have a fifty-fifty chance of springin' her loose.'

'No!' Grey felt the anger swell within him, was shocked by its intensity and listened to his own harsh words as if from a distance. 'I want Jemima home — but I also want that Indian. I want him out there, in the yard, Maddock. Naked. Pegged out in the cold wind. And when I've got him, I'm going to sit in that seat, smoking a big, fat cigar, and I'm going to watch him die.'

★   ★   ★

In the sheriff's office at Dumas, the subject of trouble between John Grey's Circle G and Deacon Wood's Wide Loop had been aired when Ford Maddock was in town, then put to one side pending developments. Marshal Jeb Horn went along with the principle of open range, which meant a man putting up fencing was asking for trouble. If another man ripped down that fencing he would meet with quiet approval from like-minded neighbouring ranchers, but if he then held on to any cattle that strayed, well, did that put him outside the law?

Everything depended, he supposed, on the man's intentions. If he aimed to hand them back to the owner then that was the end of the matter. But Deacon Wood never had been a man who was easy to understand or get along with, and by calling his spread Wide Loop he was suggesting — with some arrogance — that he was no stranger to the wrong side of rustling.

'If John Grey's keen on keepin'

Deacon Wood's cattle away from those prize bulls of his — when he gets them back — he'll fence off that ox-bow,' Deputy George Lee said. 'He'll do it again, and again.'

'Profundity don't suit you, George,' Horn drawled. 'But, talkin' of John Grey, you fancy a small wager on the fate of that gal of his?'

'Heck, I already owe you a month's wages on a passal of bets going back a full year,' his deputy complained.

'Yeah,' Horn said, 'but this time you'll be on a sure thing — and I'm offerin' double or quits.'

'How come it's so sure?' George Lee's long, seamed face was a picture of doubt, his eyes narrowed as he warily contemplated Dumas's lean, lugubrious but notoriously crafty sheriff.

'You already know the story,' Sheriff Horn said, raising an enquiring eye-brow. 'About how she rode out of her pappy's ranch on Palo Duro Creek, got took by a roving band of Black Kettle's Cheyenne and spirited off to Injun

47

Territory by a lone buck after Custer rode in?'

'So what?'

'I'm in a philanthropic mood, George — means I'm benevolent, figurin' on givin' something back to my fellow men — so in this instance I'm bettin' Jemima Grey gets herself clear away from them redskins before . . . ' — Horn squinted across the office to where a faded calendar was picked out by a shaft of sunlight — 'before Christmas.'

'Ain't *nobody* got away from them Injuns,' Lee said, amazement in his voice. 'It bein' the end of November right now, Ned, I'll take that bet. Reckon it's high time I came out showin' profit, 'stead of burnt fingers.'

Unwinding himself out of his chair, the grinning deputy spat on his palm, reached across to shake hands with the sheriff, then ambled out onto the plankwalk and headed off across the street towards the saloon.

Grinning, Ned Butt fired up a

cigarette, then skimmed his hat towards a wall-peg, lifted an untidy heap of WANTED dodgers and with a hand that was as gnarled as a mesquite thicket slid out a crumpled telegraph slip./upp

Grey girl taken by educated Indian name of Billy Sundown, he read. *Sighted by trapper heading west out of Wichita Mountains. Am in hot pursuit.*

Jim Fleet.

PART TWO

THE NEW HAND

4

They decided to ride into Circle G from the west, achieving that aim by swinging south then east to cut across Deacon Wood's Wide Loop in the hope that her arriving home from the wrong direction would take John Grey's mind off the happenings out at the Washita, make it easier for Sundown to pass himself off as a Mexican who was doing the Englishman one hell of a favour.

They rode past Wide Loop at a distance along wooded slopes that formed the spread's northern boundary, threading through the trees past a decaying cabin once used by hunters, always working their way steadily north-east and always with a wary eye on the distant buildings. Wide Loop's house and barns were of timber washed clean of colour by the pale winter sun. Dark smoke from house and bunkhouse chimneys were thin pencil-lines on the clear sky; dark specks were men, moving about the yard. And in a small corral behind the barn, two dark, bulky shapes had Jemima puzzled, then worried.

The ranch lay to the south-west of Circle G and, even if John Grey pulled down his fences, Palo Duro Creek at that location would barely provide enough dry-season water for Deacon Wood's herd. With the fences up, the neighbouring rancher's cattle couldn't reach the ox-bow and, though Jemima professed a lack of interest in her father's affairs since moving to America, she had enough intelligence to sense that Wood was not a man to walk away from a challenge.

On the ride down from Pine Bluffs she had told Sundown something of her father's plans for breeding a superior line of cattle using imported Aberdeen Angus bulls. Sundown knew that for a man to succeed at such an enterprise he would need to use unconventional methods. Those methods would almost certainly violate range traditions, and inevitably meet with strong opposition. In the West that meant warnings given in plain language, then enforced by the six-gun.

But although he knew what Jemima was thinking as she looked with frowning concern at the two bulky animals penned in Deacon Wood's small corral, once she had been safely delivered to her home, her family's concerns were not his. As he rode a few yards behind the girl's horse with the cold wind cutting into his face, Sundown knew that, in a short while, he would be hailed as a hero or a fool; he would be fêted, or hanged from the nearest tree. He had snatched the young English girl from his people because, after the experiences of his own years away, he knew that what they might do to her was wrong. But to right that wrong — to return the girl unharmed to her people — he had undertaken to deliver her to her father, and by doing so he was putting himself in peril.

He was uncomfortable in his stolen clothes, and uncertain about their usefulness. Common sense told him that there were so many hard men of all descriptions pushing into the developing West that few would give him a second glance. How could he be an Indian, a Cheyenne? He was just another sunbaked hombre dressed in black with silver conchos encircling the crown of his hat, Mexican spurs on his boots and a worn six-gun sagging at his hip. Three days' stubble darkened his jaw. His hair had been chopped raggedly short at the nape of his neck.

In appearance, he was indistinguishable from a thousand other dusty travellers.

But however hard he worked at convincing himself, Sundown knew that he was riding into a world he had touched lightly, and about which he still knew little. He was, to a great extent, ignorant of the white man's ways; John

Grey was a foreigner and so even more of an enigma and, try as he might to display confidence, Sundown knew he was doing it badly.

An hour later he rode across ripped-up fence-posts and strands of wire lying in the flattened grass, saw the ox-bow on Palo Duro Creek glistening silver in the near distance and over to his right the sprawl of buildings that he knew were Circle G, and there was the certainty within him — born of primitive instincts that no amount of time with the white man could blunt — that he was riding into trouble.

★   ★   ★

'Two riders below the ridge.'

Deacon Wood, rawboned, white-haired and bleak-eyed, was leaning with his elbows on the top rail of the corral. He turned his head, looked out across his land.

'Headin' for Circle G. You recognize 'em?'

Quent Yarrow walked over to his horse, dug into a saddle-bag and came up with a dented pair of field-glasses. He looked through them in silence, then grunted.

'A Mex, another feller in plaid mackinaw. And there's something about that Mex's horse . . . ' He shrugged. 'Ranch hands. But why here?'

Wood turned his head to spit in the dust. 'If they're lookin' for those bulls, they've found 'em — and a heap of good it'll do them.'

'If I didn't know Ramon was dead . . . ' Yarrow lowered the glasses, looked at his boss. 'That feller's got the same hat, same clothes — same everything.'

'You said it was an Indian killed him and Jake.'

'Long-haired brave, damn near cracked my skull, too.' Yarrow nodded, remembering, one hand reaching up to rub the bone behind his ear. Then he turned away, stowed the glasses, slapped his hands on his pants. 'Slit

Ramon's throat, left him naked — but I guess there's more than one greaser in these parts wearin' clothes don't belong to him.' He took his hand from his pocket, rocked it to let the silver concho in his palm glint in the fading light. 'Still and all,' he said softly, 'if I come across that feller and he's got one of these missin' off his hat . . . '

'You'll get your chance.' Deacon Wood took a last look at the two dozing bulls then came away from the corral, said, 'Let's go talk to Leroy,' and set off across the yard.

He was conscious of Quent Yarrow following him, but his mind was elsewhere, chasing through ideas he'd come up with, the plans he'd formulated, looking for weaknesses. So far, he could see none, and in any case he wasn't too concerned. Hell, he was up against an English tenderfoot and a small-town marshal used to chasing stray dogs. A man couldn't be held responsible if another was careless enough to let his prize bulls stray and, goddamnit, he had a right to move his herds to a place they could get water without tearing their hides busting through fences.

He strode past the motionless windmill, kicked open the door of the bunkhouse and went into the smoke-filled gloom. Although it was early afternoon, the oil-lamp suspended from a blackened beam was already lit, and in its smoky glow he could see his foreman, Leroy Spink, sprawled on his cot as he watched a man poking at the big iron stove and cursing.

Spink looked across as Wood entered, swung his legs off the blankets and lazily sat up. The rancher dropped onto the bench at the littered table in the centre of the room, slapped his Stetson onto the boards.

'Any coffee?'

'Comin' up.'

Spink stood, went over to the stove and, when the man replaced the iron lid with a clatter and backed off, settled the big coffee pot on the stove's top. When

60

he turned, Quent Yarrow was sitting across from Wood, rolling a cigarette.

'So . . . ' Spink sat down, the flare of the match lighting the flat planes of his face. He accepted the makings that were slid across the table, and looked questioningly at the rancher.

'There's been a lot of talk about stretching ourselves, opening up Wide Loop's horizons,' Wood said. 'Well, I can tell you, the time's come. Pop Taylor was in Dumas looking for a buyer, but the land over his way's all free range anyhow, and I've got line cabins better than his house.'

'Let me guess.' Spink's eyes glinted. 'He was drunk, and you dangled a pouch of jingling gold eagles in front of his glassy eyes?'

'All the old feller wants is out. I took hold of his arm and walked him down the street, got that lawyer feller out of bed, signed the papers so he got what he wanted there and then.'

'Money changed hands?'

'Some.'

'So now we've got us a spread on Coldwater Creek, adjoins Wide Loop and sits so close to the New Mex border the hot breeze'll carry the smell them frijoles?'

'Close enough,' Wood said, 'to put those bulls out of reach. We'll make a big show of rounding up enough steers for a drive, move them with those bulls in their midst. John Grey could be standing in this yard watching and he still wouldn't realize what was going on.'

Quent Yarrow spat a shred of tobacco, shook his head. 'Jeb Horn's a mite smarter, and George Lee don't miss much.'

'No reason for them to be around to see it happen. When that fence came down, those bulls walked onto my land. That doesn't make them my responsibility, and if they strayed once, they're likely to stray again.'

'And all this upheaval,' Spink mused, 'because a man comes in with fancy notions and fences off the ox-bow.'

'No.' Wood's voice was placid, his hands relaxed on the table. 'This move has been on the cards for some time, and you know it. All Grey's done is provide the incentive.'

'And Wide Loop?'

'Taking over Pop Taylor's land makes it a mighty big spread. Grey wants to chase his beef, he'll be on my land the whole way. That's trespass.'

There was speculation in Spinks's eyes. 'Sounds to me like you're expectin' him to do that.'

Wood shook his head. 'That's not what I want. You and Quent can ride over in the next couple of days, tell the Englishman his hunks of expensive beef were last seen heading for Kansas. If those lawmen are as sharp as you say, they'll hear about it soon enough. They'll back off, and John Grey will be out chasing rainbows.'

'What if he won't listen, comes looking? We've all heard stories about this Englishman. If they're half true, that still makes him a tough nut.'

'One man,' Wood said derisively, 'plus that new strawboss he hired, Ford Maddock, and those two permanent hands. Cowpokes. They pull a pistol they're likely to shoot themselves in the foot.'

'And with the four men we took on at Pine Bluffs we're ahead, even without Jake and Ramon.' Spinks nodded thoughtfully. 'But up to now, all that can be said is you've been tardy returning a couple of bulls that strayed on to your land. What you're suggesting is — '

'Theft? Rustling?' Deacon Wood's eyebrows were up. 'You object to that, Leroy?'

'No, sir. But I like to know what's in it for me, and I like to be sure of the odds.'

'Then do like I say. Wander over to Circle G. Leave the new men here — they can begin the gather — '

'Jesus!' Spinks said. 'They'll love that.'

'They'll do it. You get over there, tell

Grey your story. Look around.'

At the stove, pouring coffee into tin cups, Quent Yarrow flashed a look that was laced with pure venom. 'I look forward to it. Those riders up on the ridge, there's only one place they could be headin', and I'd sure like to get me a look at that feller with the Mex hat . . .'

5

John Grey recognized Jemima and began waving furiously when she and Sundown were still half a mile away from Circle G and riding in with the sinking sun a fiery crimson at their backs. Someone with sharp eyes had evidently spotted their approach, called the rancher out of the house. Now, drawing near, Sundown marvelled at this emotional reunion as the tall, lean man ran across the yard and Jemima gave a little cry of pure joy, kicked the pinto with her heels and tore away from Sundown with her soft dark hair flying.

Wearing an old hostler's mackinaw over shirt and pants, Sundown thought, and still he knows his daughter.

He rode in slowly, watching the girl draw rein in a cloud of dust and tumble from the pinto into her father's arms. From the other side of the embracing couple a tough-looking man, as brown as a nut, came across the yard. Ford Maddock, John Grey's foreman, Sundown decided, for during the ride in Jemima Grey had taken pains to give him names and descriptions. Marshal Jeb Horn and his deputy, George Lee. The rancher, Deacon Wood. Descriptions so clear he felt he knew them all. Now, like Sundown, Maddock advanced so far then held back while father and daughter allowed the grief and despair of the past two weeks to be washed away in a flood of tears.

When Sundown rattled into the yard and slid from the saddle, the first emotional tumult of their reunion had spent itself. John Grey stepped back, grinning broadly. His eyes were glistening. When he looked over Jemima's head at the man riding in, he shook his head and came around his daughter.

'Jim Fleet of Pinkertons,' he said. 'Man, you'd better step down and let me shake your hand, let me apologize for all the unjustified insults I've been heaping on your head.'

'That's not Fleet,' Ford Maddock said.

'Not Fleet?'

'I met him, once,' Maddock said, his eyes on Sundown. 'Tall, skinny feller in his fifties, bent like a willow in the wind and favoured a battered old Stetson.'

Jemima shook her head, her bright smile setting her blue eyes dancing. 'Dad, this is — '

'Mescal,' Sundown cut in quickly, stepping away from his horse to touch Jemima's arm lightly in warning.

Maddock laughed in good-natured disbelief. 'I've come across a whole lot of mescals in my time, ate them, got drunk on them times without number, even on occasion cut 'em down like weeds — but I ain't never met me a feller boasting of that name.'

'I guess my father had a wry sense of humour.'

'And I've got an English gentleman's sense of duty,' John Grey said, and stepped forward, hand outstretched.

'My name is John Grey, and I have never in my life been more pleased to make a man's acquaintance. I don't know when, where or how you did it,' he said, pumping Sundown's hand, 'but you have my eternal thanks and . . . ' He trailed off, still clasping Sundown's hand with both his own and staring deep into the other man's almost black eyes. 'And that's still never going to be enough,' he finished. 'I can't find the words, but perhaps later, when Jem's told her story and you've told yours . . . '

'John, why don't you and Jem go on over to the house?' Ford Maddock said. 'Me and Mescal can get acquainted, work out whether he's stopping a spell and — '

'Oh, he's staying,' Grey said firmly. His arm was around his daughter's shoulders. He had begun to move away, but his eyes were still on Sundown as if, Sundown thought, he was intent on burning the image of his daughter's strange rescuer on his mind. 'He's coming up to the house for dinner — you too, Ford, this is a time for celebration — and when he's eaten and drunk his fill he'll be in no fit state to climb on a horse, never mind ride.'

John Grey began laughing as he turned with Jemima towards the house, and Sundown recognized it for the deliberate, calculated response of a man who knew that nerves would snap if tension was not released. He felt echoes of that same urge within him as the danger he had anticipated was swept away like river mist by the soft winds of welcome, and with that awareness his muscles relaxed so that he strode lithely after the Circle G foreman when Ford Maddock jerked his dark head and led the way towards the low-slung bunk-house.

A couple of waddies had wandered over from the corral, and when Sundown glanced back he saw their horses being led away, and acknowledged a friendly wink from the taller of the two men. Briefly, he thought of the

Indian garments stowed in his saddle-bags, and felt a moment's unease. Then he was through the door and blinking in the gloom and stifling heat of the Circle G's bunkhouse. Light filtered weakly through dusty windows. Lanterns were cold and black on the central table. At the far end, a pot-bellied stove crackled and glowed.

'Set,' Maddock said. He kicked an iron cot, slapped dust from a corn-husk mattress and said, 'Most of the summer hands have been paid off, so you can choose where to bed down.' He grinned, in the half-light his teeth flashing white against his tanned skin. 'Close to the stove is best; too close could get you a fight.'

'We're pushing ahead of ourselves,' Sundown said. 'I brought the girl in. There's no reason for me to stay.'

'You heard Grey. The steak's already sizzlin' for you, boy, so make the most of it.'

Unease stirred within Sundown. He moved closer to the stove, aware that he was being sucked into something he hadn't wanted and didn't understand. Years in a school filled with other frightened Indian kids had seen the white man's language beaten into him with a stick and filled his mind with history that was not his own — or his own, but seen from a different and less favourable viewpoint. But here he was already being asked to stand on equal terms with men whose daily life was something he had never encountered. So far he had done nothing more than ride in, cross the yard and walk into the bunkhouse. But these were men comfortable in their own surroundings, quickly alert to anything out of place, and in Maddock's sharp eyes Sundown already detected the beginnings of suspicion.

The pot clattered as the foreman splashed coffee into tin cups. Sundown took the proffered drink, winced at the searing hot metal, reached out to place the cup on the table. As he did so the door banged open and the two waddies came in and brushed past, carrying with them the cold air of approaching winter. The tall, skinny one went to the stove. The other flipped his Stetson onto a cot and scratched a mop of red hair as he sat next to Maddock.

'This is Red, the bean-pole's Slim,' Maddock said, eyeing Sundown critically over the steaming brim of his cup. 'You, now, you're sure dressed like a Mex, but I'd say — without meaning any insult — there was Injun in there somewhere.'

'Apache,' Sundown said glibly. 'On my mother's side.'

'Maybe that explains the unshod Indian pony you're ridin',' said the man by the stove. 'But only maybe.'

Sundown's face was impassive. 'And maybe you're making something out of nothing.'

'So what is it you do, deal in horses?'

Maddock's eyes were everywhere, shifting rapidly from Sundown's face, to his hat, to the tooled leather holster, to the two men who had now settled and were listening as they sipped coffee.

'The army takes as much stock as we can deliver. Most of it's half broken. Some comes from the Indians.'

'Sounds like a good living,' Maddock said.

'Don't explain what a man who's half Apache is doin' this far north on an unshod pony,' the red-haired ranny said bluntly.

'You're not trying hard enough,' Sundown said. 'Maybe it was a replacement for a horse that went lame. Or maybe the brave with Jemima had no more use for it.' He shrugged.

'And it don't explain how he came across Jem ridin' in from the east when she was took to the west of here by Black Kettle's Cheyenne,' persisted Slim.

'There's an explanation for most things, if a man looks hard enough,' Maddock said. 'Me, I'm more interested in our friend Mescal's fancy Mex outfit,' and he reached across the table and plucked the black hat from

74

Sundown's head.

Something inside Sundown froze. He was suddenly aware that, the way he was sitting, the heavy pistol at his hip was blocked by the edge of the table; that even if his way was clear, he could not beat these men to the draw.

'I've got me a feeling John Grey's so grateful he'll offer you a job,' Maddock pressed on, 'and it seems to me you'll need to get rid of them duds, get yourself some range garb — '

And in that instant the tension within Sundown melted away as he realized what Maddock was driving at and both waddies began joshing the foreman unmercifully. The skinny man punched his shoulder and called him a name that brought the foreman half out of his chair, the red-haired fellow made a grab for the black hat and sent it skimming across the room, and Maddock roared a protest and, in ducking away, sent his cup flying and dark coffee sprayed across the floor.

'He allus was after one of them Mex

outfits,' Red said to Sundown, as Maddock dived sideways, locked an arm around the skinny man's waist and wrestled him to the floor.

'Never been the same since he set eyes on that feller works for Deacon Wood,' said the lean 'puncher breathlessly, struggling to lift his upper body off the floor, slam an arm across the foreman's chest and knock him backwards.

'Ramon,' said red-head, nodding agreement, as he watched the two men rolling in the dirt then deftly lifting his cup as they slammed into the table.

'Got a hat exactly like that one, Ramon . . . ' Slim had broken free. He bent with a grin to tousle the foreman's black hair and get his hand cuffed furiously away, then climbed to his feet and slapped the dust from his pants.

'Only that pernickety 'breed'd never've let one concho go missing,' said Red, and Sundown forced a smile to hide the sudden lurching sickness in his stomach as he recalled the scene in the Pine Bluffs livery barn, the tinkle of a silver concho on hard-packed earth, the two men who had come looking for the dead 'breed.

'Yeah,' said Slim, 'and there was me thinkin' that was Ramon's hat old Mescal here had somehow got a-hold of.'

The ruckus died down as swiftly as it erupted. Maddock recovered his cup from under a cot and refilled it at the stove, went to look for Sundown's hat and brought it back to the table.

'All of which talk is a load of nonsense and beside the point anyway,' he said, 'because all I'm sayin' is that fancy garb of Mescal's ain't no outfit for a man ridin' the range.'

They've forgotten the unshod pony, Sundown realized. But only for now. He saw the lean 'puncher settle to his coffee with a half smile, waited for the man's eyes to lift and look across the table, for the sudden shift in their expression from good humour to the open suspicion that was bound to return as he remembered his unanswered question. Before that could happen, he must . . .

'If John Grey does offer me a job — '

'He will.' Maddock nodded forcefully. He'd dusted the coveted hat, and was hanging on to it as he absently polished the conchos with his sleeve and listened intently to Sundown.

'In that case — '

'I'll trade you my Stetson.'

'Jesus!' the lean man said, eyeing the foreman's sweat-stained hat in disgust.

'And my spurs,' said Maddock. 'Those Mex rowels you're wearing'll get in the way when you're working steers, rip a good cow-pony's hide, maybe get you dragged if you're thrown.'

'Watch yourself, Mescal,' said Red, 'or he'll have the shirt off your back, and that fancy six-shooter rig.'

'Not that,' said Sundown. 'All the rest . . . ' He shrugged, and spread his

78

hands in acquiescence.

'Done,' said Ford Maddock, and before Sundown could change his mind the foreman bent and began unbuckling his spurs.

6

The room was wreathed in cigar smoke. Heavy curtains kept out the cold night air, in the background a high-horned gramophone scratchily played a tune sung by a popular female singer from back East, and silver cutlery glinted in the lamplight as silently a maid bore away the used dishes and the remains of a fine venison dinner. Standing nursing a crystal glass of whiskey with his back to the crackling log fire, John Grey was clearly a man who enjoyed the elegant trappings that were the result of his own intelligence and hard work and, from the leather chair he had been given as guest of honour, Billy Sundown gazed on this scene of imported luxury with well-concealed disbelief.

He was also careful to keep his gaze away from Jemima for, with her dark hair held high in a neat chignon and her slim figure accentuated by a simple red evening dress, she was a sight beautiful enough to tighten his throat and make him incapable of sensible thought.

And although there had been nothing but innocuous, light-hearted conversation around the dinner table, he guessed that tonight as much as in the days to come he would need all his wits about him.

From across the room, Ford Maddock caught his eye and winked. I have made a friend, Sundown thought. He has the dead Ramon's hat and spurs. He is now a smart fellow, and maybe this straw boss sees himself impressing the boss's daughter — if that's what he wants. From the foreman's behaviour during the meal, Sundown was pretty sure that was the case, and at once he felt a faint smile tug at his lips. From the moment the two men had left the dim, smoky bunkhouse and walked into the splendour of John Grey's home, Jemima's attention had rarely strayed far from Billy Sundown, and the light dancing in her blue eyes and the faint flush tinging her cheeks were a clear indication of her feelings.

Tread carefully, nevertheless, Billy Sundown told himself, for if these men ever did get close to the truth . . . And, even as that warning was impressed on his mind, he was overwhelmed by another thought that was couched as a question: even if all went smoothly, could there ever be a future together for a girl raised in England and an Indian who had already killed two white men?

Then, as if at some unseen signal, the maid cast a swift glance over her shoulder, silently closed the door behind her as she left the room, and John Grey cleared his throat.

'I took time before dinner to talk to Jem,' he began, 'so I've now got the whole story of the past worrying two weeks.' He looked apologetically at Sundown. 'No disrespect to you, young man. It's simply that I felt sure if you told the tale it would be disproportion-ately modest, and I wanted the unvarnished truth. That's what I got from my daughter and, as well as congratulating her on her courage, I'd again like to thank you, Mescal, for your swift action.'

What action? wondered Sundown. What tale has she told, and how will I pick up the thread if this shrewd man begins to ask questions? But even as those worrying thoughts crossed his mind, the rancher swiftly drained his glass and moved on.

'But thanks on their own don't amount to much. I'm sure Ford will agree with me when I say that, in our present circumstances, we can use a man with guts and determination.' He lifted the cigar, pursed his lips thoughtfully as he touched the hot ash with a fingertip and seemed to seach for the right words. 'A couple of my prize bulls strayed onto a neighbouring rancher's land when he had my fences ripped down. I believe you saw them when you rode through.' He looked up, met Sundown's gaze. 'That could be useful:

you can back me up if the marshal rides out from Dumas and doubts my word; and you know where the bulls are if we're forced to go after them.' He waited for a moment, let the words sink in, then said, 'Jem's already told me that you're at a loose end, Mescal. I'm asking you to stay on for a while. You'll be well paid for your services.'

His look was a question. Sundown hesitated for just a moment, then dipped his head in a nod of acceptance. Be like the waters of the Washita, he thought: take the route with the fewest obstructions, but have the power to overcome all if the need arises.

'That's settled, then,' Ford Maddock said as John Grey crossed the room to fill his glass, 'and we've got ourselves a new hand. But I still can't work out what the hell happened with them Injuns out there in the Nations — if you'll pardon my language, Jem.'

Grey chuckled. 'I'm sure she appreciates your concern.' He took a long draw on his cigar, blew out a stream of smoke and gestured expansively. 'A young buck decided he wanted Jem for himself, and took off with her. But like all Indians, the man was at heart a coward. Mescal was in the right place, at the right time, showed some steel, and the buck took to his heels.'

'Where was this place, exactly?'

Grey shrugged. 'Does it matter?'

'Black Kettle was on the Washita. Where in tarnation was this buck takin' Jem for Mescal to run across them?'

'He was making for the border,' Jemima said, and caught Sundown's eye. 'I think it was in his mind that safety lay far to the west.'

'That ties in,' Grey said. 'Even if Jem was unsure of her whereabouts, Jim Fleet reported that a trapper saw them heading west out of the Wichitas.'

'They made it as far as the Rita Blanca,' Sundown said blandly. 'I was riding west off The Caprock — '

'On an unshod Indian pony,' said Maddock, and Grey shot him a glance.

'You think an Indian rides a fancy

A-fork saddle?' said Sundown. 'You're making the same mistake Slim and Red made. They think there is some deep meaning in the horse a man rides. I told them: when a man's afoot, he takes what replacement is offered.'

'All right, riding west, you say — but why?'

John Grey handed the whiskey decanter to Maddock, watched him pour and said, 'You must forgive my foreman, Mescal. I don't know why he's questioning your . . . actions . . . but I do know that he's a man who came only recently to Circle G, but in that time has proved to be a man I can trust, and one without whom I would now find it very difficult to operate.'

And a man, Sundown thought, who can turn his friendship on and off like summer rain and has, perhaps, more than one face to show the world.

'I was looking for work,' he said, carefully selecting the one answer that was likely to find favour with Grey, and it was as if the tension was released from the room like air from a punctured bladder.

With a look of approval, the rancher said, 'Then it's fortuitous that you came across Jem and her rogue Indian when you did, or by now you might be on Deacon Wood's payroll instead of mine.' He took the decanter from Maddock, freshened his own drink, extended the offer to Sundown and got the same polite refusal he'd been getting all evening, then said lightly, 'By the way, Mescal, you never did tell me what happened to that Indian.'

The casual tone belied the look of naked malevolence in the man's eyes, and for an instant Sundown hesitated. Was this his chance to dump his past life on the funeral pyre? Two simple words — 'He's dead' — would convince this man that Billy Sundown had paid for his crime with his life, dispatched beyond justice or revenge by the valiant Mexican Mescal in the rescue of Grey's daughter. But what about the future? Sundown had ridden into Circle G with the intention of delivering the girl to her father, and had not thought too far beyond that. Since then he had been persuaded to stay on. That suited him, but there were imponderables, one of which was the girl's true feelings for him. He had hopes . . . but if they came to nothing, what then? He would move on from Circle G but would, perhaps, remain in Texas, so why compound the lies with one more that was unwanted, and unnecessary?

'The last I saw,' he said, 'he was hightailing back the way he'd come.' He glanced at Maddock. 'On an unshod pony.'

'Then he's out there somewhere, and if Jim Fleet lives up to his reputation I may yet see that damn redskin staked out in my yard.'

With that final, chilling comment, matters relating to Circle G business, Jemima Grey's rescue and the rogue Cheyenne were put aside, and for the next hour or so John Grey entertained the small group with a string of amusing anecdotes. When, at last, Sundown excused himself and was accompanied to the front door by the grateful rancher — who rested a friendly arm across his shoulders — it was Ford Maddock who stepped out into the night with him, clapped on the black Mexican hat and flashed a bright grin.

'Just checking, Mescal,' he said softly, as the big door shut and the two men crossed the gallery. 'And makin' damn sure the Englishman knows that story you told in there's as full of holes as an old mule-skinner's undershirt.'

7

'Too quiet,' George Lee said, and Marshal Jeb Horn cast an incredulous glance in the direction of his laconic deputy.

'Jesus, George, it's November, cold as Kelsey's ass, the man's runnin' his spread with a winter crew and his daughter's been took by Injuns. You expectin' to see a barn dance, or what?'

'I'm expectin' to see Jemima Grey settin' there like she's never been away,' Lee said mournfully, 'that's what I'm expectin'. This dang weather's chillin' my brain, makin' me fear the worst — '

'Oh my God!' Horn said with mock disgust. 'I'm saddled with a deputy with a frozen brain who reckons a few measly bucks in his pocket's more important than a young girl's safety.'

'Two whole months' wages,' Lee said with dignity.

'Right,' Horn said, suddenly grinning, 'and don't you forget it.'

He pushed on, spurring ahead of the doleful deputy with his eyes on Circle G's buildings and his breath trailing in a white stream over his shoulder. But for all the banter, and his own confidence when he had sat in his office and made the bet, he was pretty sure Jemima Grey was a long way from Texas, and very likely dead. Knowing what he knew about Indians, he hoped she was.

But that hope for a merciful end was replaced by relief, coloured by total disbelief, when he reacted to George Lee's sudden shocked exclamation. He twisted in the saddle to look where his deputy was pointing, and almost fell off his horse.

'Goddamn!' he said softly. 'She *is* back — and she ain't learned her lesson.'

The dark-haired young woman was thundering up from behind to cut across their approach at an angle, lithely riding a glistening thoroughbred mare that could have been the twin of the one lost when she was taken by the Cheyenne. She was pushing the horse hard, and as she raced by some fifty yards in front of them she turned her head, flashed a gleaming smile of pure joy, and they were left to wallow in the dust of her passing.

'Looks like Jim Fleet's been chasin' moonbeams, or tellin' tall tales,' Lee said.

'Maybe not. Up to now we've had a couple of wires, and what he said in the last was he was closin' in, had high hopes. Now, if the gal's here, who d'you suppose brought her in?'

They were approaching the Circle G yard, hooves clattering on the hard earth. And, Horn was forced to admit, there was very little activity. As they skirted the empty corral he saw Ford Maddock coming out of the bunkhouse and angling towards the house; saw John Grey start across the gallery from his front door and stop at the steps to look across the yard. But of the two permanent hands, Slim Garratt and Red Quinn, there was no sign, and Horn thought again of the young girl on the thoroughbred, and the little help she could expect if things again went wrong.

'Don't pay me yet,' Horn said, as George Lee's horse pulled alongside and nudged his leg. 'Chances are that gal'll be a prisoner again before she's much older.'

'If lightin' strikes twice in the same place,' Lee said, 'which it don't.'

'It has been known,' Horn said shrewdly, 'even if it ain't the same fork.'

Then John Grey had recognized his visitors and was down the steps and striding across the yard to meet them.

'Good morning,' he called.

'From what I've just seen, it looks like it is,' Horn said as he slid down and let the reins trail.

Grey smiled. 'All right, Marshal, your disapproving tone has been noted. But Jem's had enough of her freedom being restricted, and circumstances are favourable, surely?'

Horn stripped off a glove and shook the rancher's hand, then cocked his head questioningly. 'Favourable how?'

'Well, Black Kettle's Cheyenne have been tamed by Custer, right? — and the man who brought Jem in claims he sent that redskin packing.'

'Jim Fleet?' George Lee said, and turned to make a lugubrious show of searching the yard.

Grey laughed. 'That's the mistake I made yesterday. No, this man is half-Mexican. He came across Jem and the Indian when they were making for the border.'

'Who says?'

'Why, he did. Mescal.'

'Why would a Cheyenne want to cross into New Mexico, Mr Grey?'

'Why not?' Grey eyed the marshal challengingly. 'I hear he's an intelligent man, used to white ways. He'd seen his tribe take a beating. He couldn't go back.'

'With the whole of Injun Territory to roam in, he didn't need to.' Horn spat, pulled his glove back on, glanced across at Grey's strawboss. 'You swallow that tale?'

'Not without question,' Maddock said.

'Me neither,' Horn said, and looked at Grey.

'I wasn't quite accurate,' Grey said. 'The story actually came from Jemima,' and Horn knew the rancher was now daring him suggest that his daughter was, at the very least, an unreliable witness.

He sighed. 'This Mex, is he still around?'

'He's on the payroll.'

'That's not exactly answering the question,' Horn said.

'He rode out early with Slim and Red,' Maddock said. 'Deacon Wood still ain't showed up with them two stray steers,' he added, wooden-faced.

Horn's lips twitched. 'If they strayed onto his land, he's under no obligation to do so.'

'This story gets repeated ad nau-seam,' Grey said impatiently. 'The bulls strayed because Wood tore down my fences. He was not within his rights.'

'A lot of men would dispute that.'

Grey laughed without mirth. 'They'd be as wrong as Deacon Wood.'

Still in the saddle, leg cocked over the horn as he rolled a cigarette, George Lee said, 'Sounds to me like you expect Wood to bring your bulls back, Mr Grey.'

'I do.'

'But from what Ford just said, I'd say your three men have rode over there to brace him.'

'They've ridden in that direction, yes?'

'God almighty!' Jeb Horn said. 'Are you going to volunteer any information? What are they about to do? Steal those bulls back?'

'Keep a weather eye open.'

'Now, to an Englishman that might make sense,' Jeb Horn said, ' — but what the hell does it mean?'

'When my daughter skirted Wide Loop on the way in with Mescal, she's pretty sure she saw the bulls in Wood's corral. I want to know if they're still there.'

'If they're not, they'd surely be on their way back here — or do you suspect otherwise?'

There was naked cynicism in John Grey's eyes. 'Marshal, that man has in his possession two bulls worth a small fortune on their own, a much larger fortune in their potential progeny. He has an awful lot of land, room to manoeuvre, and the law in these parts can cover only so much ground. Now, in his position, what would you do?'

'He's got more than you know,' Horn said. 'Word is he bought out Pop Taylor, and that extends his land damn near to that New Mex border.'

★ ★ ★

Jemima Grey clattered into the yard half an hour after the two lawmen left for the long ride back to Dumas. Her cheeks were flushed, and with a quick wave to her father she rode straight into the open barn to tend to the lathered thoroughbred.

Ford Maddock had wandered away towards the end of Jeb Horn's visit. Now, he crossed the yard to the house, knocked on the door and went in with his fancy Mexican hat in his hand.

John Grey was over at his roll-top desk, riffling through a sheaf of papers in the light of an oil-lamp.

'Ford?'

'You reckon Horn should have ridden over to Wide Loop, confronted Deacon Wood?'

'It would have been logical, perhaps, but not helpful.'

'Right. No crime's been committed, so him and George Lee'd be wasting valuable time.'

'And rounding up stray cattle isn't Marshal Horn's job.' Grey dumped the papers, slammed on a brass paper-weight and swivelled away from the

98

desk to eye the foreman.

'You uncomfortable about this?'

Maddock shrugged. 'You know my feelings about fences. That means I've got some sympathy with Wood. But I don't go along with rustling, and if he hangs on to those bulls much longer he's treading a mighty thin line.'

'Instinct warns me he's already committed to the wrong side of that line. If so, he won't take kindly to visitors. I told Red to take care, observe from a distance.'

Maddock nodded. 'It's been done before now. A good place'd be that old cabin, in the timber, up on the ridge overlookin' Wide Loop.'

'Right. Red had the same idea. He's taken my field-glasses, gone the long way round. He'll go no closer than the cabin.'

Grey turned as the door slapped open and Jemima came in with her face flushed and a spring in her step.

'What cabin, Dad?'

'The old Clancy place,' Grey said.

'Ah, we passed it, yesterday.'

'Yeah,' Maddock said. 'You and Mescal.'

Jemima frowned. 'And what's that supposed to mean?'

'It means the boys were talking, and a lot of what they said makes sense.'

'About . . . about Mescal?' She saw Maddock register the slight hesitation, and rushed on, 'Talking about what?'

'About this and that,' John Grey said. 'Man talk. Leave it, Jem, go on through and get your bath.'

She pursed her lips, and cast a last, lingering glance at Ford Maddock before going through to the kitchen.

'That'll be the third or fourth hot tub she's soaked in since she got home,' John Grey said. 'Still trying to wash off the stink of those Indians — '

'What she's tryin' to wash off ain't on the surface,' Maddock said. 'And I reckon she's thankin' God her pa's an Englishman.'

Grey frowned. 'Meaning?'

'A white woman unlucky enough to

get caught by Injuns can kiss her family goodbye, 'cause they'll disown her. Best thing she can do is pray the redskins never let her go or, if they do, hold her head up high and take a long, last walk into the desert.'

For a long moment there was silence as Grey stared into space, his lips tight, the knuckles of his right hand white as bone as he gripped the paperweight. Then, in a voice without colour or tone, he said, 'Is it any wonder that what I want more than anything is to get my hands on that Cheyenne and . . . '

He blinked, took a deep breath, deliberately pushed away the paperweight and flexed his fingers. When he spoke again, his voice was back to normal. 'What were we talking about, Ford?'

'You were saying Red'll go no closer than the Clancy cabin. So why three of them?'

'There's nothing for Slim to do here. He went along for the ride. And Mescal needs to see the lie of the land.'

'Why? What are you planning, John?'

'My plans haven't changed. How I carry them out may have to be adjusted.'

Maddock waited, then shook his head in despair. 'I can understand Jeb Horn's chagrin. You don't give much away, do you?'

Grey's smile was the briefest change of expression, there, then gone. 'All right. Bluntly, I don't intend to throw good money after bad. That means we recover those bulls and, as they say in this country, Wood can have it easy, or hard.'

He turned back to the roll-top, found a sack of Bull Durham and tossed it to Maddock, then took a cigar out of a wooden box and with a hard snap cut off the end.

With a haunch on the arm of a chair and his hands busy rolling a smoke, Maddock said, 'Seems an unlikely coincidence, Wood buyin' out old man Taylor only days after those bulls strayed.'

'Pah!' Grey struck a match, lit the cigar, leaned across to light Maddock's cigarette. 'There's no such thing as coincidence. Wood already had plans, my bulls came along and gave him a kick in the pants.'

'You know that?'

'I know businessmen the world over. I'd stake my life on it.'

'Yeah, and I know the West.' Maddock trickled smoke. 'So what have we got? A man keen to expand gets the chance of doublin' the size of his spread. At the same time, pulling down a length of fencing — '

'Which he had no reason to do if he was expanding westwards along the Coldwater.'

' — gives him possession of a couple of prize bulls. What comes next?'

'That's obvious. Destroying that fencing was calculated — '

'You're saying the bulls didn't stray?'

'Right. And now, with all that land, and unlimited water, he can move them around as he pleases. Keep them out of sight. Breed from them.' This last was said with venom, and he managed to instil anger into the simple act of flicking ash from the cigar.

'Which brings me back to that same question,' Maddock said, watching the lean rancher. 'What are you planning, John?'

'I told you — '

'No. Recovering them, either easy or hard, tells me nothing. I told you I know the West. What you've got is a winter crew — Red, Slim, me — '

'And Mescal.'

'Yeah, right. But if there's even the smell of trouble, Deacon Wood will have done some hiring. I reckon that's why Quent Yarrow was up in Pine Bluffs. In fact, I can't see any other reason why Wide Loop men'd be there.'

'Two of his hands were killed in a fight.'

'And their places filled, twice over. I'll bet my boots on it.'

Cigarette smouldering between his fingers, Maddock stood up, crossed restlessly to the window, turned with the light outlining his dark frame.

'All that means,' Grey said easily, 'is we're outnumbered. But with the right intelligence, and the element of surprise, small forces win battles. Red will come back with information. We can use that to — '

Hooves rattled in the yard. Maddock swivelled, reached to sweep the curtain aside, swore softly.

'Riders!' he said. 'And they ain't ours.'

8

Five miles west of the ranch the two Circle G men and the new hand veered sharply north, cutting well away from the Wide Loop boundary and holding that course for another couple of miles before again pointing their horses west, on a line that would bring them to the tree-covered ridge that formed Deacon Wood's northern boundary and was already familiar to Sundown.

The early sun was at their backs, but with barely enough warmth to clear the morning mists. Every so often Slim drew rein to sweep the terrain to the south through John Grey's field-glasses. Once, when they had again been heading west for almost an hour and had reached the timber slopes, he grunted and handed the glasses to Red. They said nothing to Sundown, but his sharp eyes, unaided, were able to pick out the distant specks that were two riders heading east from Wide Loop.

'Maybe they'll stop short of Circle G land,' he said, letting them know he was missing nothing, and Slim shot him a glance.

'Maybe. Could be checking to see if that fencing's back up.'

'So's they can hitch a rope and pull it down again,' Red said, and looked at Sundown.

'Sounds like grown men playing a game meant for children.'

Red shrugged. 'Ain't a whole lot for a man to do with nothing but grass as far as the eye can see.'

'Explains why Deacon Wood's holdin' on to them bulls, and why Maddock's eyes lit up when he saw that fancy Mex hat you were wearin',' Slim said.

'And why he took it — same way you did,' said Red.

'No,' Sundown said, and knew that these men would be harder to convince than an English rancher blinded by emotion and gratitude. 'It was my hat, for a long time.'

'Naw.' Red shook his head. 'And you ain't no Mex, and you didn't ride no unshod pony all the way from . . . ' He cocked his head. 'Where was it you said you was from?'

'San Carlos,' Sundown said. He picked the name out of vague memories, and at once sensed his mistake.

'Close to four hundred miles.' There was naked disbelief in Red's eyes.

'And you keep making the same mistake. The horse I rode from San Carlos went lame. The unshod mount was a replacement. Like this one.' He patted the big dun's neck, the mount from the Circle G cavvy he had been offered and accepted and that now bore his acquired A-fork saddle and saddle-bags.

Slim had taken the glasses from Red and was again sweeping the grassland to the south. Without turning, he said, 'Maybe I keep gettin' all mixed up because you and that Injun pony you left in the corral make a better match.

108

Maybe it's because nothing you say adds up — like where you came across Jem, what you were doin' there — and that goddamn name.' He let the words hang in the chill air, then switched tack and said, 'Red, looks to me like Wide Loop's doin' a gather.'

'In winter?

'Don't make sense.'

'Damn right. Though maybe friend Mescal wouldn't know that.'

Sundown laughed dismissively. 'But of course the Cheyenne know cattle — '

'Didn't you say you was half Apache?'

In the sudden silence, Slim stowed the field-glasses and swung his horse.

'Aw, let it rest,' he told Red. 'You can shoot his story full of holes, but the plain truth is that one way or another he brought Jem back home.'

'Yeah, and why is it, when I wonder why, I get this picture of a dog sniffin' around a bitch — ?'

'Cut it out!'

'You're wrong,' Sundown said.

'I don't think so,' Red said, 'but right now we've got a loco rancher doin' a roundup in the middle of winter and the only way we'll find out why is — '

'By asking him,' said Slim.

'You think he'll tell us?'

'He'll tell us where to go,' Red said.

'Because he knows you're Circle G,' Sundown said. 'But he doesn't know me, so why don't I ride in?'

'You?'

Sundown spread his hands. 'At the house, last night, John Grey said I could be useful. He was right. I've seen the bulls, I know where they are. Now you need somebody to get closer, learn more.' He touched his sweat-stained Stetson. 'Thanks to Maddock, I now look like a cowhand.'

'Driftin' through, lookin' for a meal?' Slim nodded slowly. 'Why not?'

'A thought just occurred,' Red said, and when Sundown looked into the 'puncher's suspicious eyes he knew that Red was about to put into words what he himself had been contemplating as one of his better options. 'We let Mescal go, I don't reckon we'll see him again.'

'I agree, but for a different reason,' Slim said. 'If Wood gets suspicious, he's liable to take Mescal and go lookin' for a tall tree.'

'If he's half as suspicious as you fellers,' Sundown said, 'I don't stand a chance.' He stared at Red, forced him to avert his gaze, then looked at Slim. But the lofty cowhand was a horse of a different colour and, far from being abashed, he gave voice to intelligent and considered misgivings.

'Naw, you'll get by,' he said, 'because it seems to me you've been deceivin' us ever since you rode in with Jem — and that makes the gal part of it, and I can't figure out why. Anyhow, you've got kinda good at playactin', and as it's John Grey and Circle G you're fooling, I reckon you've got more to worry about from your new friends than from Deacon Wood.' He looked levelly at Sundown. 'And I guess that little mouthful has made damn sure you

111

head West at a fast lick as soon's we turn our backs.'

* * *

But he didn't.

The two Circle G riders were still within sight through the sparse pines as he reached the old cabin and looked back along the length of the slope. As if sensing his gaze, Slim turned in the saddle, lifted a hand. He stayed that way, awkwardly twisted, watching, waiting, and with a crooked smile Sundown pointed his horse downslope and headed for Wide Loop.

The sprawling buildings that made up Deacon Wood's spread were no more than a mile to the south, half hidden by the stubborn mist that was clinging to the lowland like a thin, much-torn grey blanket. Another half mile and Sundown was in it, and the icy touch of the clammy air was so reminiscent of the last day at the Washita that he heard again the brassy blare of bugles, the excited howls of Custer's cavalry above the rattle of gunfire, the panicked screams of the Indian children — and he drew rein as a shiver racked his muscular frame.

What was he doing here? Why had so much changed since he slashed open the wall of the tepee and rode away from his people with Jemima Grey? At the time, his reasons had been clear, and impelled by the vicious dawn raid of the 7th Cavalry: what his people would do to the white woman if she remained their captive indefinitely was wrong, and she stood little chance from Indian or white man in the mindless violence of that calculated attack that had turned into a massacre.

But, since then, each step he took seemed to develop in directions that were beyond his control: he had searched for clothes in the white-man's town, and had killed a man; he had handed Jemima Grey safely to her father, and somehow agreed to stay on;

he had ridden out in the morning light with Slim and Red, and was now committed to a leading role in . . . in what? In a senseless feud between two white men over the ownership of pedigree bulls.

Why?

Again, that simple question.

It was haunting him, for in the end there was only one answer and it lay in his first sight of a young girl with eyes as blue as summer skies and the raw emotions that had swelled within him at the touch of her hands on his neck as, exhausted, she used his sharp blade to cut off his hair and her soft words to give him her trust.

And it was taunting him, because the naked suspicion from all sides that caused his skin to crawl at his own vulnerability was warning him that this white girl was forever beyond the reach of an Indian.

Or was she?

Billy Sundown eased his weight in the saddle, registered the lazy creak of leather in the morning silence, reached absently to touch the chill damp coating the horn.

He could not go back. Black Kettle was dead, his people dead or dispersed. The reasons that drove Sundown away from the Washita with Jemima Grey were still valid, and were daily being reinforced as the Indian nations faced the final defeat. If he could not go back, nor could he remain still; he must go forward. And when that realization came unbidden to his mind, the question haunting him changed from why, to how, and was somehow less daunting: *why* asked for reasons but would give nothing in the answer; *how* called for decisions that would lead to action.

As the mists that had clouded his thinking were swept aside to reveal hope, those blanketing the ground were lifted and dispersed by the freshening breeze. Now, from half a mile out, Sundown could clearly see the corral. The two bulls were there, the yard and the ranch buildings beyond them silent and still. In his short spell at Circle G he had already learned that, at summer's end, ranchers paid off most of their hands and retained a skeleton crew. Through his glasses, Slim had seen two Wide Loop men heading in the general direction of Circle G, others out rounding-up cattle. So, how many did that leave?

At that moment an idea stirred within Billy Sundown, one so outrageous that it at once became feasible: as an Indian, he knew that the element of surprise was a valuable weapon, and the more unexpected the attack, the greater the shock. Shock removes a man's ability to react. If Deacon Wood was alone, sudden awareness of his perilous situation would intensify the shock. By the time he recovered . . .

Deliberately, Sundown took a deep breath. He had nudged the horse into motion and was now nearing the yard, but, while his horse moved at a walk, his heart was dangerously outpacing his brain. Given the advantages, over-powering a lone rancher should not be difficult. But to remove John Grey's two bulls from Wide Loop — there, it was out, the idea naked in his mind with all its many weaknesses exposed — meant pushing them east across Wide Loop land. In that direction, Wide Loop riders were gathering cattle, others perhaps done with range chores and swinging their mounts for the return ride.

Then, with a suddenness that snatched away that vital element of surprise and, in the instant, stripped from Billy Sundown the veneer of a white man and left revealed the naked savage, a man stepped out of the barn and into the yard.

The Sharps .50 he was holding was rock steady, and pointing at Sundown's head.

9

Quent Yarrow was not only a good judge of horseflesh, he had a mind that kept a vivid record of almost every mount he had seen, or ridden. So when he followed Leroy Spink into the Circle G yard, sight of the horse tossing its head in the corral rang bells not once, but twice: he had seen that horse before, on two previous occasions — and this third sighting jogged his memory.

John Grey was out of the house and watching them as they rode in. Ahead of Quent Yarrow, and unaware of what was occupying the other man's thoughts, Spink half turned to say, 'He's unarmed. Back me up, nothing more,' then pushed on across the yard to wrench his horse to a dusty, sliding halt alongside a gleaming top-buggy.

'If you were my foreman, and rode

like that,' John Grey said, 'you'd be cleaning that buggy, then collecting your pay.'

'Yeah, well, we don't take kindly to powder-puff riders at Wide Loop,' Spink said. Yarrow slid from the saddle, loose-hitched his horse to the buggy's near wheel and stood, thumbs hooked in his belt, confronting the rancher.

'Where'd that horse come from, Grey?'

'Horse?'

'Come on! You've got an Injun pony in the corral. I saw it in the livery barn at Pine Bluffs, saw it again crossing Wide Loop range. Now it's here.'

Grey's lip curled. Deliberately ignoring Yarrow, he turned to Spink. 'If you've finished showing off, tell me what you want, then get out.'

Spink shook his head. 'Hellfire, Quent, ain't that something? We bring a feller news of his valuable stock — and he insults us.'

Yarrow nodded abstractedly, his eyes busy.

'There's a man hiding in the house.'

'Hiding?' Grey's lifted an eyebrow quizzically. 'From you?'

'So, what then? The curtains moved. If that ain't hiding, he's being pretty cautious over his watching.'

'Maybe,' Leroy Spink said, 'he's that new foreman, makin' sure we don't rough up his boss.'

'You might bear that in mind,' Grey said to Yarrow, with a significant glance at the pistol slung low on the Wide Loop man's hip. Then, to Spink, 'What's this about my stock?'

'You want them missin' bulls,' Spink said, grinning, 'tell Slim and Red, to head towards Kansas.'

'Which means exactly what?'

'Means Deacon Wood got sick of babysittin' your beef, and turned them loose,' Yarrow said. Then, hitching up his gunbelt and glancing restlessly across the gallery towards the window, he said, 'Tell him to come out.'

'Maddock!' Grey's face was tight as he half turned and shouted to the house. Then, his attention back with Yarrow, he said, 'What the hell do you mean, turned them loose?'

'Yarrow's just joshing, Grey. Those two bulls got themselves loose, lit out for the north ridge. But I reckon he's right about Kansas, if they keep runnin'.'

'You're lying,' Grey said, then turned as boots sounded on the gallery. Ford Maddock was out of the house and walking towards the steps, hat in hand. 'You listening to this, Maddock? D'you believe one word of it?'

Maddock came down the steps, planted his hat on his head, opened his mouth to speak — then froze as Quent Yarrow's six-gun came out and the hammer went back with an ominous click.

'Well, now,' Yarrow said.

'Lordy,' Leroy Spink said with deep irony, 'somebody just turned up wearin' old Ramon's hat.'

'You, feller, pouch that pistol,' Maddock said curtly.

'I don't think I can do that,' Yarrow said. 'I've got a good memory for horses. If that's your pony in the corral, you were in Pine Bluffs the back end of last week.'

'Your memory's failing. I was in Pine Bluffs, sure, but that's not my horse. Now put up that pistol.'

'And not your hat.'

'Wrong.'

Yarrow took a breath, shook his head. 'No, I'm not wrong. It was dark in the livery barn. You've had that long hair chopped short, but I don't forget a face. You'd've passed for a 'breed — wearin' his clothes you could've been Ramon, back there in the shadows — but when we'd loaded the bodies on a buckboard we found — '

'Ford Maddock is my foreman,' John Grey said.

'Since when?' said Leroy Spink, easing himself away so that the straw boss's attention was dangerously split.

'None of your damn — '

122

'When!'

'A few days. Long enough for me to get to know him.' Grey gestured angrily. 'What's the man supposed to have done?'

With the pistol still lined up rock steady on the fuming foreman, Yarrow reached into his vest pocket. 'What he's done,' he said, 'is lose a concho off Ramon's hat,' and with a quick flick of his thumb he sent a glittering disc of silver spinning into the dust.

Maddock's eyes dropped, lifted. Suddenly, in his manner and posture, there was the tenseness of unease.

'For God's sake!' John Grey said. 'Tell him, Ford.'

'Yeah,' Yarrow said mockingly, 'tell me how you took a likin' to them Mex duds, stripped off — '

'He got the hat from a man called Mescal,' Grey said, 'the 'breed who brought my daughter home.'

'Across Wide Loop land,' Yarrow said, and waggled the pistol. 'I watched them. Through glasses. It was him.'

'Not him. I told you. A man called Mescal — '

'So where is he, this 'breed?'

'He rode out with Garratt and Quinn.'

Yarrow's laugh was a bark of disbelief. His suppressed anger was rising. His knuckle whitened on the trigger.

'Easy, man,' Ford Maddock said. Under the rim of the black hat, fresh sweat glistened on his forehead.

'Me and Ramon joined Wide Loop together,' Yarrow said. 'Along with Jake, we rode up to Pine Bluffs to sign new hands. Ramon got drunk, wandered over to the livery barn. This feller . . . ' — again the pistol waggled — 'this feller broke Ramon's neck, took his clothes.' He turned, spat onto the hard earth. 'We had words with the old hostler. You know you hired an Injun, Grey? And did I neglect to tell you he also stuck a knife in Jake's throat?'

'Don't be ridiculous — '

'The old hostler saw it all,' Yarrow

said, and now he seemed to be gathering himself, stoking up the fires that would burst into violent action. 'But I don't need his word. I looked into this feller's eyes when he leaped across that barn and felled me with a single blow. Hell, look at him, he's a goddamn redskin — '

He broke off.

Words were like bullets spat in rattling volleys by Grey and Yarrow. In the fierce exchange, and as his anger rose, Quent Yarrow's attention had wavered: his hot gaze had moved to the rancher, his pistol still centred on Maddock's chest, but drooping, and the Wide Loop waddy's finger had slackened on the trigger as his mind drifted elsewhere.

All this was noted by Maddock. The Circle G straw boss chose his moment, and took his chance.

In a blur of movement and a whisper of sound, his hand dipped and his six-gun snapped up. Away to one side, Leroy Spink yelled a warning and went for his gun. John Grey was caught flat-footed, his mouth open. Yarrow jerked back to life and pulled the trigger. The crack of the shot was followed by a second as Leroy Spink fired.

But Maddock had moved, leaping backwards and down to roll as his pistol came clear of leather. Yarrow's slug, intended for his chest, hummed on across the gallery and shattered a window. The shot fired by Spink chipped splinters from a rail and sent them whirring like deadly needles as Jemima Grey stepped out of the front door.

Close by and crowding, the two horses snorted, then moved in a wheeling, flashing dance that kicked up a cloud of choking dust and rocked the top-buggy.

Grey roared, 'Jem, get back inside!'

Spink yelled, 'Girl, you stand still!'

Then the two Wide Loop men were ducking and weaving as Ford Maddock rose up from the dirt and used the hard edge of his palm to fan the hammer of his pistol and send hot lead screaming across the yard. Spink tripped and went down with a yell as his spurs tangled. A slug sent his hat spinning. Quent Yarrow spat a string of curses.

John Grey, jolted into action by his own shout, had stepped behind the top buggy. Jemima went back into the ranch house and the door slammed.

In that instant, with the hard slap of wood on wood, the yard went silent.

Ford Maddock stood with a look of puzzlement on his face as he frowned at his pistol. Then, as the horses snorted uneasily and the top-buggy creaked, his jaw tightened. He flipped open the chamber of his six-gun and made a fumbling grab at the filled loops on his gunbelt.

As he did so, Quent Yarrow grinned, and casually planted a bullet in the Circle G straw boss's heart.

Maddock went backwards as if kicked by a horse. He was dying on the way down; dead when he flopped like an empty sack in the dust.

Then Jemima burst from the house. Her blue eyes blazed a cold and furious fire, and in her capable hands she was carrying a shotgun.

10

'I know you, don't I?'

The Sharps was held low across Deacon Wood's body, but Sundown could see that the hammer was back and it would take but an instant for this powerful, grey-haired cattleman to swing the rifle and squeeze the trigger.

But he has just the one shot, Sundown thought, and I will be an elusive target. And with that shot wasted and the empty Sharps occupying his hands, the pistol at his hip will be useless.

He had ridden across the yard with his body coiled like a spring, his eyes fixed on the man with the Sharps but his peripheral vision alert for other movements, his ears attuned for the slightest sound. He was rewarded by silence — nothing stirred in the barns, or the bunkhouse — then the soft sounds of nature as a breeze whispered through the branches of the tree in front of the house, and one of the big bulls lowed in the corral.

With the threat of danger from other quarters removed, Sundown advanced across the yard, his full attention now on the man with the rifle. As, across the narrowing gap, he sought out the man's eyes, he surmised that this rancher saw nothing to fear in the lone newcomer, but was habitually cautious. Nevertheless — out of his own habitual caution — Sundown met those eyes and looked hard into their depths for it was there, in those mirrors of the soul, that the man's intentions would be betrayed.

And when the question came, larded with uncertainty — 'I know you, don't I?' — it was the eyes and the sudden, shocking memory of their blank indifference as hard boots sank into the fleshless ribs of children in exile, that told Sundown this man was not mistaken: they knew each other, and Deacon Wood could never be trusted.

'No.' Sundown forced a thin smile. 'You don't know me. I'm here by chance. Riding through when those two bulls caught my eye.'

'Really?'

'True.' Sundown drew rein and rested his hands on the horn, the dun's damp muzzle now almost touching the cradled Sharps. 'A man doesn't pass up the chance of getting close to such fine animals.'

The rancher took a pace backwards. 'That what Grey told you to say?'

Sundown tilted his head. 'Grey?'

'Step down.'

Sundown came out of the saddle in one smooth movement, and landed like a cat. A quick slap sent the dun trotting across the yard, and he saw the man take note of these actions, saw the eyes register the fact that they were now standing in open opposition with nowhere to hide — and saw the sudden curl of the lip and the sudden fire in those eyes as this born fighter caught the whiff of battle.

Deacon Wood shook his head, and shrugged. 'If I don't know you, I know of you. You're Maddock, John Grey's new straw boss.'

'I don't know John Grey, or this man Maddock.'

'You're lying.'

'And you are talking big for a man on his own.'

Wood grinned, and waggled the Sharps. 'This makes me big, Maddock.'

'Makes you *feel* big,' Sundown said. 'If I am Maddock, why am I here?'

'Grey wants those bulls. If he's going to take them, with my men out on the range this is the best chance he'll get.'

'But how would he know about this situation with your men?'

In Wood's eyes there was sudden impatience, irritation. 'A stranger would ask what the hell I'm on about. You're conducting a goddamn interrogation. Why? Because you're Maddock. How do I know? Because I can use field glasses the same as Slim. Him and Red were up there with you, at Clancy's cabin. You rode down. Where'd the others go?'

Sundown shrugged, realizing that any further subterfuge would be useless, but that this man was overconfident and at his mercy. 'Away from here. Back to Circle G.' Again the shrug, this time with hands lifted and palms spread, done deliberately to distract, to draw the man's eyes.

And the eyes wavered, jumped to the hands, then back to Sundown's face with sudden understanding of his slip.

'Right. Now we come to it: you're Maddock, there's only one damn reason you'd come here, so unbuckle — '

'Not Maddock,' Sundown said. He pitched his voice hard and high, shocking Wood; shrugged yet again; spread his hands and watched the rifle begin to swing around and, in a continuation of the wide-armed gesture, dropped onto his hands with his body kicked out straight and used his stiff foreams as a pivot to bring both legs around in a flailing sweep that

133

scythed Wood's legs from under him and threw him down hard on his shoulder.

The Sharps spun away to land on its butt, the jolt dropping the hammer and sending a bullet hissing skywards. Before the echoes of the shot had died away, before Wood could move a muscle, Sundown doubled, plucked his knife from his boot and used the power as he uncoiled to spring onto the downed rancher. One fist took a twist of shirt as the forearm slammed Wood hard down on his back. The other hand brought the sharp blade in fast to press against the slack skin under the older man's chin, slid the warm metal a fraction to slice and draw blood.

'Not Maddock, but Awakening, the young Cheyenne who was schooled by the Quakers and was a target for your boots,' Sundown said, and his dark eyes were inches away from the blue eyes as, with sinews of steel, he held Wood pinned while the stunned rancher sifted through the ashes of old memories and

finally registered disbelief, then awareness, then bleak resignation.

'A goddamned Indian kid,' Wood said
huskily, and with a swift hollowing of
the cheeks he gathered saliva and spat
in Sundown's face.

Soundlessly, Sundown shifted his
weight and rolled the rancher onto his
face, ripped his shirt sleeve clean off at
the shoulder and used the cloth to
bind his wrists, then again turned him.
Straddling the bucking form, he bent
forward, wiped the spittle from his
face on Wood's chest, caught the tang
of his cold sweat and let the
amusement show in his eyes as he
sprang clear and the rancher wriggled
away, using his heels in the dirt for
leverage, to stop ten feet away, panting
and watchful.

Feeling the eyes on him, Sundown
picked up the Sharps by its muzzle
and smashed it against the ground. He
tossed the shattered butt in one
direction, the blued barrel in another,
crossed to the dun and listened to

the familiar brittle rattle of turkey quills as he took a strip of rawhide from beneath the clothing in a saddle-bag. Then he went back to Wood, took him by the shirt and dragged him through the dust of his yard to the big tree. There he hauled him to his feet, jabbed the point of his knife under the rancher's chin to force him up on to his toes, and held him in that position by binding the rawhide tight around his throat and securing the loose end to the jagged stump of a low branch.

Then he dismissed the white man from his mind, turned, and looked across the yard and beyond the barn to the corral.

So, could it be done?

And if he succeeded in returning the bulls to John Grey, what then?

In his thinking on the way into Wide Loop he had reached the conclusion that he could not go back to his own people. Black Kettle was dead, all Indian nations doomed. But much had happened in a few short, violent minutes. His reactions when confronted by Deacon Wood had been the reactions of an Indian. His treatment of the man when he was defeated had been the sanguinary treatment that would be meted out by an Indian.

But if this awareness suggested that going the white-man's way was too alien, and would be too fraught with difficulties ever to work, the alternative was to ignore the existence of Jemima Grey — and he could not do that, would not do that. Driven by strong emotions he had plucked the white woman from the grasping hands of murderous squaws, had risked his life for her in the face of the advancing 7th Cavalry; had killed for her, in cold blood.

Last night, in the panelled luxury of her father's house, he had believed that what he saw in her eyes was an emotion that matched his own. It could be that he was mistaking gratitude for love — but he thought not. It could be that what he saw shining in those blue eyes was hero-worship — but, again, this was something he could not accept.

But even if what he saw in Jemima's rapt gaze was something deeper than the mere reflections of his own powerful feelings, he was still left with the yawning gulf that separated the races, and the same question: the return of the bulls would find favour with John Grey and make more acceptable anything that might develop between the man Mescal and his daughter — but what then?

For a man and a woman to come together, and live together, there must be the twin bonds of respect, and trust. For the union of a man and a woman of different races to be accepted, there must be the respect and trust of their contemporaries. He had Jemima's trust, but her respect could be scattered like the husks of dry leaves in the fall if she learned of the Pine Bluffs' killings; from the white men he had met, all he had

138

received was thinly veiled suspicion.

The wet sounds of a man gagging cut through his reverie, and he turned to see Deacon Wood straining to rise onto the tips of his toes as an instant's relaxation threatened him with strangulation. And — as if standing outside his own body, watching, yet unable to interfere — Sundown knew that if anything could bring home to him the impossibility of what he had been contemplating in the harsh days since the Washita, it was his reaction to this situation.

What he did — as he watched without surprise — was to turn and look with absolute indifference at a man who was fighting for his life. The red face and protruding eyes registered on his consciousness, but evoked no sympathy, nor any other reaction. He watched incuriously as Deacon Wood achieved a position that allowed him to breathe. The colour suffusing the rancher's face drained away to leave it filmed with cold sweat. His back was stiff against the tree's trunk, his chin jutting, his eyes closed, his thigh muscles quivering.

But to Sundown it was as if the man were part of the tree and, because the tree was of no use to him, he turned away with his mind at once intent on other matters.

To move the bulls from Wide Loop to Circle G, he would need rope for halters. He would find that in the barn. If the Wide Loop men were between him and Circle G, he would need to avoid them by taking the long way round. He at once thought of the cabin on the ridge. Because Texas was strange to him, he should follow known trails, and he had ridden the ridge twice in two days. Also, it was possible that Slim and Red had hung back, curious to see what he achieved.

All this passed through his thoughts as he gathered the dun's trailing reins and walked the horse across the yard towards the barn. But he had covered less than half the distance when the drum of hooves came to his ears, and he was cursing himself for a fool when two horsemen came pounding along the east trail and into the yard and caught him flatfooted.

11

They'd ridden no more than four miles south of Circle G on the return to Dumas when George Lee looked across a tangle of mist shrouded chaparral away to his left and said, 'Rider coming.'

Jeb Horn grunted. 'Frettin' about that bet you lost is seriously eroding your limited efficiency, George: I've been watching that feller for ten minutes.'

'So've I,' Lee said, smirking. 'For fifteen.'

'Then now he's close enough to plug us both if he so chooses, maybe you can enlighten me as to his identity?'

Lee frowned. With a tightening of the jaw he hitched his pistol into a handier position, took another squinting look north-east as the approaching horse-man picked a way through the scrub and said, 'Well, he ain't comin' from Wide Loop so he's prob'ly not one of Deacon Wood's men, we've just left Circle G — '

'So he don't work for John Grey,' Horn cut in, savagely mimicking his deputy's drawling voice, 'but if you had your wits about you and had been listening to Ford Maddock you'd have figured out by now that this feller who looks too old and hungry to stay in the saddle must be Jim Fleet.' He waited for the thought to sink in, then softened the barb by saying, 'Jim and me met up at the end of the war, seen each other once or twice since, so I guess I've got the advantage.'

The man who brought his big, lathered chestnut alongside the two lawmen was predominantly grey, bent like a sapling too long in the wind and with a battered Stetson pulled down tight to touch ears like jug handles. But the look in the grey eyes was penetrating and shrewd, and in their depths a light danced as he nodded at Jeb Horn.

'Well met, Jeb.'

'Saved you a ride, have I?' Horn leaned out of the saddle and grasped the extended hand. 'George Lee here, my deputy, he had you spotted a while back. I guess you left your caution back in the Nations.'

Fleet nodded to Lee, and grinned. 'I've learned to watch my back, leave the front to take care of itself.'

The three men had pulled their horses off the trail. Once again, George Lee hooked his foot around the saddle horn and began rolling a smoke. Jeb Horn watched the Pinkerton man cross his hands on the horn and ease his lean frame in the saddle, noted the weariness in the man's naturally gaunt countenance. And he thought of what had transpired on the way into Circle G, and the conversation with Wood pertaining to his daughter's return — and wondered how much Jim Fleet knew.

'You ridin' in to report a success, Jim?'

'Nope. I figured I was gettin' close to that redskin and the woman, then came across something in the woods told me I was chasin' moonbeams — '

He broke off as George Lee chuckled so hard he blew out the match flame, cocked an eyebrow at Horn, got a non-committal shrug in return and dismissed the deputy with a wave of the hand.

'Or chasin' my own damn tail,' he continued, 'so I figured I'd best — '

Again he broke off, glowering, but this time in response to Horn's raised hand.

'Before you tell me what you found and what you'd best do,' Horn said, 'let me bring you up to date. Jemima Grey's back home with her daddy, brought in by a 'breed name of Mescal. They claim — Mescal and the girl — the redskin was heading for the New Mex border when this Mescal hove up and rescued her. Last seen, the redskin was headin' back towards the Nations.'

Jim Fleet pursed his lips, sucked his

teeth, and slowly shook his head. Without seeming to look, he lifted a hand and caught the tobacco sack thrown his way by Lee.

'You see this Mescal, talk to him?'

'He'd rode out early, with a couple of Circle G hands. I spoke to John Grey.'

Still looking sceptical, Fleet rolled his cigarette, fired it, trickled smoke. He squinted one-eyed at Horn.

'I found a campsite,' he said. 'Naw, a stop-off, in the woods east of Pine Bluffs. Sign said there was two horses, one went off towards town, came back. There was a woman's dress tossed in the bushes, ripped, bloodstained . . . ' He let the words drift into silence, waited, took a pull at the cigarette, gazed patiently off into the distance as if watching the mist fight a losing battle with the weak morning sun.

'And?' Jeb Horn said.

'And a stinkin' buffalo skin, some hanks of black human hair,' Fleet said.

'Injun hair?' George Lee said.

Fleet shrugged, glanced questioningly at Horn. 'Grey tell you what his gal was wearing when she rode in?'

Horn exhaled heavily. 'I can see where this is headed. If that was her dress you found she got a change of clothing. One of them rode into Pine Bluffs, so . . . '

'Two Wide Loop men died in the livery barn, one with a broken neck, one knifed,' Fleet said. 'The one with his neck broke was a 'breed, favoured fancy Mex garb. He was stripped naked. The hostler saw it all. The killer was an Indian, long hair, a tough young buck. He saw him strip, put on the Mex clothes; was held at gun-point, forced to give him a couple of saddles, a shirt and pants, an old mackinaw.'

'Well now,' Jeb Horn said. 'Remind me, George, what was Ford Maddock wearin' when he came into town about them bulls?'

'Range garb,' Lee said.

'And when we rode into Circle G — as I recall — he came across the yard with a fancy pair of Mex spurs jinglin' and a black hat on his head all sewed up with conchos.'

'Timing's wrong for it to be him,' Jim Fleet said.

'Sure. But this Mescal, now, if he likes changing clothes to cover his tracks . . . '

Fleet nodded. 'John Grey's English. Could be he doesn't realize what's going on. Let's go tell him.'

PART THREE

BILLY SUNDOWN

12

John Grey was using tweezers to pick the last splinter from his daughter's face when Horn, Lee and Fleet came thundering into the yard. He heard the racket, dropped the wet cloth into the tin basin of hot water and said quietly, 'Wait here, my sweet.'

When he eased open the front door and looked out across the gallery, the three horsemen were out of the saddle and casting about the yard where Ford Maddock had fallen.

As the echoes of the shot that killed the straw boss had faded away to leave a stunned silence, Jemima had screamed her despair from the doorway and let loose with one barrel of the scattergun. Shot hissed high above the two Wide Loop men. Mockingly, they had raised their hands as if to ward off an evil spirit, then piled into the saddle and hammered out of the yard.

Maddock was beyond help. Between them, Grey and Jemima had dragged him into the barn and laid him to a temporary rest in fresh straw. But his dark wet blood still stained the dust, the gouged tracks where his heels had trailed across the yard drew a graphic picture and, as Grey watched, George Lee said something to Jeb Horn and started towards the barn.

'Trouble, Grey?'

Grey shook his head ruefully at the marshal's question, gestured vaguely towards the retreating deputy. 'Wide Loop men killed my foreman. Leroy Spinks, Quent Yarrow. We put him in the barn, but . . . '

'Why would they do that?' Horn flashed a glance at Fleet, led the way up the steps onto the gallery and, as the rancher advanced to meet them, said, 'Grey, this is Jim Fleet of Pinkertons, the man who was out there in the Nations looking for your daughter.'

Grey shook hands with the gangling

Pinkerton man. 'You have my thanks,' he said quietly, 'even if, in the end, your efforts came to naught.'

'Not entirely,' Fleet said.

Grey hesitated, then tightened his lips and shook his head. 'You'd better come inside.'

The big room was gloomy in the wan light of a winter's day, the single oil-lamp casting its glow over the table and the bloodstained water in the bowl, its reflection dancing on Jemima's marked face as she dabbed it with a dry cloth.

'Splinters,' Grey said. 'One shot hit the door frame, I suppose you could say Jem was lucky.'

'Ma'am.' Fleet touched his hat brim, Horn doffed his Stetson and held it in front of him. Grey gestured vaguely towards chairs, waited until the visitors were seated, then said, 'Clearly, something's happened to bring you back.'

'You can blame me for that,' Fleet said. 'And I can understand how, with your daughter back with you and all, you figure the affair's over. But her bein' home's only part of the story. A couple of men died up in Pine Bluffs. Seems somebody was after a change of clothes, and it all went wrong.'

'What were Spink and Yarrow doing here, Grey?'

'They told me my bulls have strayed again. I didn't believe them.'

Horn nodded. 'You know it was Wide Loop men died in Pine Bluffs?'

'It was mentioned.'

'Why?'

Grey frowned. 'I don't understand,' he said, and Jim Fleet exclaimed softly.

'They came about your bulls,' Horn said. 'What brought up the killings?'

Metal tinkled as Jemima dropped the tweezers into the bowl and carried it through to the kitchen. The door closed quietly behind her. Grey glanced over that way, then back at Horn. There was a new, darker light in his eyes.

'It was a case of mistaken identity,' he said. 'Quent Yarrow was in the livery barn in Pine Bluffs when those men were killed. He mistook Ford Maddock for the . . . for the killer.'

Horn smiled crookedly. 'Those aren't the exact words you were about to use.'

'He was going to say this Yarrow mistook Maddock for the Cheyenne buck,' Jim Fleet said. 'They told you it was an Indian did the killing, didn't they?'

'Yes, they did, but they were wrong about Maddock — '

'Why would they make that mistake?'

'Maddock's got — had — the right features. One of the men killed was a 'breed. He liked to dress like a Mexican. Today, Maddock was wearing a Mexican hat — '

'A lot of them about,' Fleet said.

Grey took a deep breath, let it out slowly, looked down at his clenched fists. 'This one had a concho missing. Quent Yarrow had a concho in his pocket, seems he picked it up in the Pine Bluff's livery barn.' He opened his right hand, tilted it, let the lamplight wink on the silver in his palm.

'Where's the hat? With Maddock?'

Grey shook his head. 'Yarrow took it.'

'When Maddock was in town to report the loss of your bulls,' Horn said, 'he wore a Stetson looked worse than mine. So where'd he get the Mex hat that came off a dead Wide Loop rider?'

A shadow fell across the room as George Lee came through the door. He eased himself to one side, listening. John Grey poked the silver concho with his finger, held it and sent it tinkling onto the table. His eyes were ugly.

'From Mescal.'

'For God's sake, Grey!' Horn said. 'You're actin' like a man with his head stuck in the sand. You must have had your suspicions before Quent Yarrow confronted Maddock. Hell, your gal was taken from the Washita by a Cheyenne buck, she comes home in the company of a man who tells you he's half Mex and sent that redskin packing and — '

'He brought Jem home,' Grey said tightly.

'His name's Billy Sundown,' Jim Fleet said flatly. 'On the way in he killed two men up in Pine Bluffs.'

'Custer and his cavalry killed women and children to rescue other white prisoners.'

'Indians,' Fleet said. 'Regrettable, but done in the heat of battle. This was cold-blooded murder.'

'He brought Jem home,' Grey said through clenched teeth. 'When I knew an Indian had taken her, I wanted more than anything to see him there, in the yard, staked out, dying. *But he brought her home . . .*'

Jeb Horn sighed.

'Last we heard,' George Lee said from the door, 'he was out Wide Loop way with Slim and Red.'

'We could mosey over,' Horn said. 'See what the hell Deacon Wood's playin' at with those bulls.'

'And most likely find this Sundown's moved on,' Jim Fleet said.

'No.' Grey shook his head.

'So what's holdin' him here?'

Grey said nothing. The question hung, unanswered.

'Ah,' Jeb Horn said.

'Something between him and the girl,' Fleet said, looking at Grey. 'And she's likely been takin' in everything we've said.'

'Yeah,' Jeb Horn said, looking at the rancher. 'And she walked out five minutes ago — so where d'you reckon she is now, Grey?'

13

The two riders came into Wide Loop at
a gallop; in rapid, sweeping glances took
in the drama being enacted in the yard
and peeled off to either side, dragging
their mounts to a slithering, spinning
halt. Pistols cleared holsters. Metal
flashed in the cold air.

Their shouts of surprise and the
sudden clatter of hooves spooked
Sundown's horse and with a determined snort it wheeled away, ripping
the reins from his hand. And suddenly
the skittish horse was thirty yards from
him, trotting with head high and eyes
rolling towards the house and the big
tree where Deacon Wood was fighting
to stay alive.

'Stand still! Get your hands high!'

Exposed, covered by cocked pistols
aimed from two directions, Sundown
felt his lips peel back from his teeth in

an instinctive, animal snarl.

But even as he hissed his hatred, he was exploding into action. In two pumping, high-kneed paces he burst from standstill to dead run. He launched himself at the moving dun from behind, planted both hands behind the cantle and went up over its tail in a vault that carried him into the saddle. The first shot kicked up dirt between his feet as he left the ground. He felt the wind of the second as he reached down for the trailing reins and drew back his arm to snap them tight and spin the horse towards the danger. Both his heels slammed into its ribs and raked hard. His heart swelled with a fierce joy at the instant, muscular response. Then he was down, flat along the dun's straining neck, squinting ahead through the streaming mane.

He rode straight at the rider on the right, saw his horse's ears flatten as it squealed and began to rear, saw the man make a grab for the horn and swing his pistol. Even as the shot cracked and the muzzle flashed Sundown slid effortlessly sideways, falling to curl along the dun's side supported only by a sinewy leg crooked over the saddle, a hand clamped on the horn. In that position he drew his pistol. From under the dun's neck he snapped a shot. The man jerked upright, and went backwards out of the saddle.

As he went down, his horse leaped sideways in fright and crashed into the second rider's mount, almost unseating him and sending his pistol spinning through the air. In that instant Sundown again turned the dun. He drove it hard at the two milling horses. It bore down on the startled rider who was kicking at his partner's panicking horse and fighting to stay in the saddle. Out of sight, a burr clinging to his horse's flank, Sundown precisely calculated his move. The riderless horse broke clear and trotted away as Sundown's dun pulled alongside the unarmed Wide Loop rider. Like a spring recoiling,

Sundown went back into the saddle. Using the momentum to carry him on he flung himself at the other rider, hooked an arm around his neck and swept him from his horse.

Somehow they twisted in the air. Sundown hit the dirt on his back, underneath the other man. But he was taut, braced, and even as the man's weight came down, Sundown was reaching up with both hands to grasp his shirt front and throw him to one side. Then, cat-like, Sundown was on him. One leg went over to straddle the downed man. One hand slapped viciously to snap his head sideways, the other slid into his boot. The knife flashed. The blade leaped to touch the man's throat, the sharp point settling on the skin under the plaited rawhide cord that secured the black Mexican hat with the missing concho.

'No!'

The man's eyes were wild. And now, from close up, they were eyes Sundown recognized, eyes last seen in the cool dimness of a livery barn as he used the hilt of this same knife to pound this man into unconsciousness.

'What happened to Maddock?'

'I . . . he's dead, I . . . '

Sundown looked into the man's eyes and saw the sudden panic as, with all the power of a blow to the stomach, he was hit by stark realization: the wild-eyed Cheyenne buck he thought he had killed at Circle G was holding a knife to his throat. His face a mask of indifference, Sundown shifted the knife and snicked through the chin strap, heard the man's choking gasp as the hat was knocked into the dust and Sundown grasped a handful of hair and pulled hard back and to the side so that the hairline was exposed.

'Jesus, no!' the man moaned, and began to buck.

Within Sundown, blood pounded hotly as conflicting emotions raged. His thighs were clamped, the man's head held hard against the dirt. He could move, but go nowhere. The agony of

Sundown's hand savagely twisting his hair brought tears to his eyes. One smooth, circular sweep of the blade would remove his scalp. One slash across the throat from ear to ear would put a terrible end to his agony.

But something stayed Sundown's hand, held the knife steady even though a primaeval instinct was screaming at him to thrust and slash, to take his bloody prize.

He had killed two men in the Pine Bluffs livery barn for the sake of a suit of clothes. At Wide Loop another — who had mistreated him in the past but here had rightly and nobly been protecting his property — was suffering torment as he strained to stand tall enough to breathe and would surely die if not released. This man held helpless beneath him would — if Sundown used the sharp knife — die choking in agony in a widening pool of his own blood.

These were white men. They were the men for whom he had forsaken his own defeated tribe, the all-conquering people he must live with — if he was to continue living; the compatriots of the beautiful young woman whose trust — and perhaps much more — he had won by displaying admirable qualities of fast thinking and bravery.

How long would that trust last if he killed this man and allowed Deacon Wood to choke to death? How long would it last, anyway, if Jemima Grey were to discover that his quick thinking and bravery masked an Indian's innate ruthlessness; that the clothes Sundown wore on the long ride home had been taken from a man whose neck he had broken; that the clothes that kept her warm had been given to him by an old hostler as another man lay gurgling his life away with blood pouring from the terrible knife wound in his throat?

So the dilemma he faced as he straddled Quent Yarrow and held the knife's point hard up against the man's quivering flesh was this: if his hard-won standing with Jemima Grey was, and always would be, precariously balanced — why go on? If he was born a Cheyenne and would always be a Cheyenne, why force himself on the white men when, in the end, it would come to naught?

Because, he told himself, he had come this far and there was no turning back. Black Kettle was dead, murdered at the Washita. The Cheyenne were finished.

Yet even as his logical brain began immediately to question his arguments and ask him why, why could there be no return to the past, to the life he had known with his own kind? — the frustrating mental impasse became redundant as the rapidly swelling whisper of distant hooves again attracted his attention.

Yarrow had heard that distant drumming. The light in his eyes changed from fear, to hope, then back to naked panic as pressure on the needle-sharp point biting into his

166

throat increased and he saw Sundown's eyes narrow, his teeth bare. But the knife's movement had been an unintentional reaction to the sudden movement as Sundown straightened and cocked his head to listen. The man held helpless between his clamped thighs was forgotten, the mind that had been occupied with questions to which there was no answer had moved on and, as the whisper of hooves swelled to an ominous, hard drumming and he knew that the Wide Loop range riders observed by Slim and Red were returning home, Sundown sprang lithely away from Quent Yarrow.

With four men riding in like the wind, the odds were too great. He looked around for the dun, saw it standing with the other loose horses, whistled softly and saw its ears prick. He met it as it came towards him, leaped into the saddle and bent to pouch the knife. His last image as he rode away was of Quent Yarrow scrabbling across the dirt towards his fallen six-gun.

Then Sundown was clear of Wide Loop and once again riding towards the ridge where an old-timer's cabin offered sanctuary.

14

He felt as if the life he had left in ruins on the banks of the Washita had melted away like the snows of his twenty winters and was now so distant that it was beyond memory, the new life he had chosen slipping further out of his reach with each hour that passed.

He had tethered the dun on the edge of trees fringing a patch of grass, then kicked open the door of Clancy's cabin and entered the mouldering interior. The weather had destroyed the roof, turned the floor to slime and heaped dead leaves against all four walls; the iron stove was a heap of rust, blankets mouldering rags on an old wooden cot, the table missing one leg. But the gaping windows overlooked the steep slope of the ridge and the sprawling buildings of Wide Loop, a weak sun had cleared the mists of morning, and from that excellent vantage point he watched and waited.

Nothing moved. He had seen no-one since his hurried departure from the ranch.

His flight from Deacon Wood's spread had taken him well away from the approaching riders. Someone — probably Quent Yarrow — had blasted two wasteful shots after him when he was beyond six-gun range, but the sounds of expected pursuit had never materialized and the wide half-circle he had ridden to avoid the Wide Loop men had seen him urge his horse up the distant end of the ridge and approach the cabin from the west.

It was a repeat of his ride home with Jemima Grey, but he had rarely felt so alone.

He guessed that pursuit had been delayed because of the need to free Deacon Wood — or perhaps they thought a rogue Indian not worth the trouble. Cutting the rancher loose and removing the dead man would have been done while he was approaching the ridge and making his way to the cabin. After that, Wood and his crew had dispersed, and were now in either the house or the big barn, or perhaps in the bunkhouse outside which the new arrivals' horses were hitched.

But what would they do next?

Deacon Wood was holding John Grey's bulls. The man Quent Yarrow had killed Grey's foreman. When Yarrow gave that news to Wood, the rancher would know what to expect: John Grey would come after the bulls, and the killer — but would he come alone with Slim and Red, or enlist the help of the law?

A sudden flurry of activity drew Sundown's gaze towards the bunkhouse, and it at once became clear that Deacon Wood was not prepared to wait. Four men came out, a motley bunch looking more like gunslingers than 'punchers, with pistols worn low and holsters tied to their thighs. They went to the horses at the hitch rail and untied

171

their lass ropes. Then Yarrow emerged, carrying a rifle, his gaze lifted to rake the landscape to the east. He was followed by Deacon Wood, who crossed the yard towards the house. The four men with ropes headed for the corral, followed more slowly by Yarrow. He watched them go in and slot the bars behind them, then strolled over and leaned on the top rail, watching.

The bulls were about to be moved.

Then another movement attracted Sundown's eye, away to the east. A single rider, at that distance seeming scarcely to be moving but, to his sharp eyes, obviously pushing the horse hard and heading straight for Wide Loop.

Jemima!

Sundown put a hand on the window's rotting sill and vaulted through. He squatted on his heels, let his eyes settle and adjust and watched the girl gradually loom larger as the distance between her and the ranch narrowed.

He pondered, thinking of possible reasons for her lonely ride and what she intended — and, at once, the answer came to him.

If Slim and Red had returned to Circle G, they would have told John Grey that the man Mescal had gone in alone. That information would also have reached Jemima. But how would she react to the news that Sundown, the man her father knew as Mescal, was again involving himself in his affairs and could be in great danger?

Sundown believed that there was a bond linking them — understood yet never put into words — that had been forged when he snatched her from the bloodbath that was the Washita, immeasurably strengthened when he had fulfilled his promise to bring her home to Circle G. He knew that if ever she learned of the sanguinary ruthlessness that came as second nature to him, the resilience of that bond would be tested to breaking point. But until then, she would feel an obligation to him that would be difficult to resist — and a girl who had no qualms about riding alone

173

on the range was by nature single-minded, and impulsive.

Even witnessing the killing of Ford Maddock would not prevent her doing what she considered to be her duty: the man who had rescued her from the Cheyenne, and from Custer's rampant cavalry troopers, could not be abandoned.

But, Sundown thought with a heavy heart, when she set out from Circle G she could not have known that the ruthlessness born in me has again been manifested in an outburst of violence, and that violence has changed everything for all time. It will, quite soon, change my image in her eyes, but before that it will affect her reception at Wide Loop: Deacon Wood is himself a ruthless man, and the arrival of Grey's daughter at his door will place a deadly weapon in his hands.

And now the girl was no more than half a mile away. The men in the Wide Loop corral were fully occupied, as too was Quent Yarrow. There was no sign of Deacon Wood.

Sundown came quickly to his feet and drew his six-gun. His eyes fixed on the girl, he fired a single shot into the high, thin clouds. The crack of the pistol seemed puny against the immensity of the open range, but the oncoming horse slowed and Sundown could clearly see the girl's head turn as she searched for the source of the sound.

He stepped forward, lifted his arms above his head and waved them slowly from side to side. Still the horse pressed on; slower, yes, but still heading for Wide Loop, and danger. A few hundred yards ahead of her the trail wound around a low bluff. From there, she would not be seen from Wide Loop. But now, too, the men in the corral had paused to watch and listen — and now, by the tall tree where he had recently faced an agonizing death, Deacon Wood was looking towards the ridge.

Sundown's eyes narrowed. The girl was pushing on. She had not seen him.

Patiently, he fired a second shot. She was closer now, so the sound reached her faster and with greater urgency. This time she hauled on the reins and pulled the horse to a halt, and when he again stood tall and waved his arms, he saw the sudden pallor of her face as she turned to look directly at the cabin.

Then, with the impulsiveness that had driven her from the Circle G to look for the man known as Mescal, she swung the horse away from Wide Loop and spurred up the long slope.

★   ★   ★

They met Slim and Red three miles out of Circle G, paused at the side of the trail to fill them in on the cold-blooded murder of Ford Maddock by Quent Yarrow, the conversation Jemima had heard — which had colourfully embellished Ford Yarrow's earlier comments in the yard — and her reaction. She was in the house, John Grey said, then she was gone, and a quick search outside

176

for her horse confirmed what he had feared: she had ridden out, and as to her destination there was only one conclusion to be reached.

Somewhat shamefaced, Slim sneaked a glance at Red then admitted they'd seen Leroy Spink and Quent Yarrow riding west and kept well clear, a good while later watched Jemima Grey pushing her thoroughbred in the general direction of Wide Loop and figured she was on one of her wild rides. They'd passed within a couple of hundred yards of her, given her a wave, and let her go.

'Damn the both of you!' John Grey said.

'What's done can't be altered,' Slim said. 'Maybe she is lookin' for that Injun, but if Mescal's worth his salt he'll be on his way back here herdin' them two bulls.'

'He's a killer name of Billy Sundown,' Jim Fleet said. 'And if he has got his head screwed on he'll know his masquerade's doomed to failure

— most especially at Wide Loop.'

'A few of Wood's hands were still out on a gather — I counted four — Spink and Yarrow no more than halfway between here and home,' Red said. 'That puts all six of Deacon Wood's men away from the spread, and him on his own for a considerable spell.'

'Then I pray for him,' Jim Fleet said, and as George Lee breathed a fervent 'Amen' they all paused for sombre reflection.

John Grey broke the silence.

'A second wrong doesn't right the first,' he said, 'but if Deacon Wood does pay a hard price, then for what he and Yarrow have done I'd say it's no more than he deserves.'

'And if he doesn't,' the Pinkerton man said, with unassailable logic, 'then it's because Spink and Yarrow and those other fellers all get back home sooner than expected. They do that, the Injun might have no time to play fancy games with that toothpick he used up in Pine Bluffs — and that don't bode well for Miss Grey.'

'Agreed,' Grey said. 'I don't put it past Deacon Wood to use whatever or whoever he can get his hands on, so let's waste no more time,' and he was already swinging his mount when Jeb Horn held up his hand.

'Seems to me every man hereabouts has his mind all tied up with an Indian who could be a dozen miles away and heading for home — '

'I thought he was sweet on the girl?' Fleet said. 'Besides, he ain't got no home, 'less it's on the Red. What's left of Black Kettle's band moved there, along with the Arapaho.'

'Don't bother me where the hell they're at,' said Horn. 'Like I say, maybe he's gone, but if he's still around I'll take him in for the murder of that Wide Loop 'breed — '

'Ramon,' said Slim.

'And either way I sure as hell am going to arrest Quent Yarrow for the murder of Ford Maddock, then have a quiet talk to Deacon Wood about those fancy steers he's holdin'.'

He parried the black look thrown his way by John Grey with a sardonic grin thrown over his shoulder as he eased his horse back onto the trail. The rest of them followed, and the three lawmen and the boss and crew of the Circle G pulled a spreading plume of dust behind them as they thundered across the range towards Deacon Wood's Wide Loop.

★   ★   ★

'That's Jemima Grey,' said Quent Yarrow.

At the sound of the shot he had left the dusty, sweating men in the corral and crossed the yard to join Wood. There was a streak of drying blood running down his neck from the small puncture, a matching streak of blood and an ugly red weal under Deacon Wood's chin the rancher was thoughtfully rubbing as he gazed up towards the ridge.

'What the hell is she doing here?'

Yarrow shrugged. 'She was heading this way, changed her mind at the Indian's signal. Maybe there's something between them. Why else would a Cheyenne turn his back on his people and bring a white woman home to Texas?'

'Killing two of my men on the way,' Deacon Wood said with tightly suppressed fury, 'then coming here to kill my foreman and maul me with his filthy hands.'

Yarrow nodded absently. 'Those bulls are proving difficult,' he said.

Wood shot him a look. 'Meaning?'

'Getting them ready for the move west could take time. You're tying up four men on a job with no urgency, when you should be thinking about Jeb Horn.'

'Me?' Wood's laugh was a bark of contempt. 'You shot an innocent man for wearing the wrong hat. If Horn comes, why shouldn't I just hand you over?'

'It ain't your way, and it don't fit in with your plans. Like you said, Leroy Spink is dead. That leaves me, and those four useless six-gun drifters chasing two big bulls around a corral with lass-ropes. I'd say that makes me foreman — and what I also say is that gal up there is going to draw her pa and his crew here with Horn and Lee. That shortens the odds, makes them close to even.'

'In my book,' Wood said, 'evens means the result sits on a knife-edge.'

'So we'd best be ready.'

Wood grunted. 'You're suggesting I go against the law to save your skin.'

'Look at it from a different angle: if you refuse to hand me over, Jeb Horn will try to take me by force. When the bullets start to fly, you'll have your chance to put Grey out of the way for good.'

'That still leaves Horn and Lee like two thorns in a cougar's paw.'

'Does it?'

Wood looked at the gunman, at the

clotted blood on his neck, at the murderous light in his eyes, and nodded with grudging approval.

'Maybe Leroy Spink getting himself killed did me a favour,' he said, almost to himself. 'Grey out of the way gets rid of a minor irritation. With Horn and Lee gone I'd have considerable respite, and by the time Dumas town council get around to swearing in a fresh lawman . . . ' He paused, again touched his throat, glanced up at the ridge. 'But I don't believe in taking chances, and we should learn what we can from those damned redskins. When they face defeat, they see nothing wrong in running away. When they attack, they don't believe in forewarning their enemy.'

This time it was Quent Yarrow who was momentarily puzzled. Then, seeing the look of cold steel in the rancher's gaze, he said, 'If that means what I think it means, we're going to take the whole damn bunch of 'em from ambush soon's they ride into the yard.'

'Are you up to it?'

'And when that's done, go after the Indian?'

Deacon Wood's mouth had drooped into a cruel, downward curve.

'Go get those fools out of the corral.'

15

'I came quickly because I thought you were in trouble,' she said.

'Some. But it was soon over.'

'How?'

'The men who caused it were forced to change their minds.'

'Are they alive?'

'Two of them.'

'And the third?'

They were outside the cabin, lost in the shadows against a front wall damp from the mist and cold. Jemima Grey's thoroughbred was ground-hitched on the grass close to Sundown's horse. In the girl's troubled, questioning blue eyes he saw not disbelief, but trepidation. He believed that she was telling the truth when she gave her reason for coming after him — but not all of it. And he guessed that Quentin Yarrow had done some talking before he killed the man wearing the black Mexican hat.

Yarrow had been in the livery barn at Pine Bluffs. He had looked into Sundown's eyes, taken a blow to the head, and later regained consciousness to see the bloody, broken bodies of his companions. If, at Circle G, he had conveyed that information to Grey when Jemima was in a position to overhear, then it was as Sundown had anticipated, and feared: Jemima Grey wanted, more than anything, to believe that the Wide Loop killer was lying, but her violent experiences at the Washita suggested strongly that he was telling the truth.

The answer to this question would not convince her either way. He would tell the truth, but it was already another mark against him, another nail . . .

'He died. Two men came, with guns. I shot one, subdued the other.'

'That takes care of two. But you said three.'

'The other was Deacon Wood.'

Sundown shrugged. 'I dealt with him first, when I was going after the bulls.'

'How?'

Again the shrug. 'You don't need to know. But he is alive.'

'And unharmed?' And now Sundown saw something in her eyes that went beyond trouble. An understanding. No, the beginning of understanding. And, perhaps, a realization of what lay ahead, and what she must do.

A movement caught his eye, and he gestured with a sweep of his arm towards the long slope and, beyond it, the Wide Loop yard. 'There. With Yarrow. You see him? Deacon Wood.'

She nodded. 'What are they doing?'

'More important,' Sundown said, 'is what your father will do.'

She smiled, but it was a painful smile. 'There are three lawmen. One works for the Pinkertons. He was notified as soon as we left the Washita, listened to rumoured sightings, picked up our trail after we left Pine Bluffs. The others are locals, a marshal and his deputy from Dumas.'

All the while he was watching her, and it struck him that if she was of his people he would know how to handle this, for there were traditions, and those he understood. But she was not of his people, and so he was like a man feeling his way through woods at night, never knowing when a wrong step would bring an unseen branch whipping across his face.

'What did you overhear?' he said.

'From Yarrow?'

'Then. Later.'

'He said that in Pine Bluffs an Indian killed his friend and stole his clothes. That he also killed another man.' Like Sundown, she was carefully watching the movement in the yard at Wide Loop, the occasional flash of weak light on cold steel. 'Did you do that?'

'It was unavoidable.'

'Is that why you let Ford have your hat? To distance yourself from what you'd done?' She hesitated, then said softly, 'To allow somebody else to take the blame . . . to die for your crime?'

He shook himself irritably, came away from the wall to look down at Wood's spread, then into the east where the light was fading; where something moved, in the near distance; from where, faintly, too faintly to have reached the girl's civilized ears, came the whispering sound of approaching hoofs.

'I asked you what your father would do. And now it is important, because you see, down there, you see what they are doing?'

'He'll come after me. The lawmen, Horn and Lee, will come after Yarrow. And I think the Pinkerton man, Fleet, would like to take you back to Pine Bluffs.' There was flat despair in her voice, and he thought that he should go to her, touch her — but he did not know how. 'No, I can't see,' she said. 'You tell me. What are they doing?'

'They are preparing an ambush. And — '

He broke off as he saw the sudden

awareness in her face, caught the sudden turn of her head as, now, she picked up the sounds of the approaching horsemen.

And before he could stop her she had run across the grass slope to the thoroughbred and was in the saddle, a fancy plaited quirt rising and falling as she drove the big horse back down the slope at breakneck pace to intercept the extended line of riders now approaching Wide Loop, and headed by her father.

★   ★   ★

'Hold up!' Jeb Horn called.

The lead rider turned his head, saw Horn gesturing and slowing and all the riders coming together in a bunch, and pulled his horse back to a trot. Quickly, they joined him, and the six riders milled in a tight group as the white vapour rose in clouds from the sweating horses.

'Now we're here, no sense riding in

like madmen,' Horn said, as John Grey eyed him with irritation. 'Like Slim said, they've been out on some kind of roundup, but we've seen no sign of life and my guess is the whole crew's settin' there waiting.'

'All right, then it's ground of their choosing,' John Grey said. 'But we're a match for them, and backed by the law.'

'That doesn't carry much weight. This is a different time, a different place, unlike any skirmishes you might've experienced,' said Horn.

'Not so.' Grey shook his head. 'I was in India at a savage time, yet even there the sudden appearance on the scene of men in authority has been known to quell violent uprisings.'

'Don't take bets on that happening here,' Jim Fleet said.

'Just supposing you're right, and they don't respect your badges,' Grey said with a curl of his lip, 'what do you suggest?'

Horn was silent for a moment as he gazed ahead. The east trail hit Wide

Loop on a curve, snaking in to the left of a low, tree-lined bluff that was a smaller version of the distant ridge. Beyond it, the ground opened out quickly, dipping gently into the yard proper with its house, bunkhouse, barns and corral. Because of the low bluff, approaching riders might be heard, but could not be seen.

'I'll ride in with George,' Horn said. 'Wood knows the both of us by sight, so when we get there his reaction'll tell us what mood he's in.'

'If they're waitin' like you say,' Jim Fleet said gravely, 'that bluff's got enough cover to hide a small army.'

'The alternative,' said the marshal, 'is to stand here and holler till we're hoarse, or all go home.'

'I think you're building a major war out of minor squabble,' Grey said. 'He's holding two of my bulls, and one of his men has committed a serious crime. I'm sure he'll see sense.'

'Maybe. But while me and George are riding in, I want Slim and Red out wide on the flanks, you and Jim Fleet coming in not too far behind.'

Grey shook his head. 'Oh, all right, if that's the way you — '

'Rider coming,' Red Quinn said.

She was racing towards them at an angle, the thoroughbred stretched out as it came off the slope of the ridge and cut across the flat grassland to the east of the low bluff. John Grey grunted as he recognized horse and rider, separated from the group and went to meet her. While the others watched, father and daughter exchanged words. When John Grey returned with her to the group, his face was expressionless.

'It seems you may be right. Wood and his men have been preparing some kind of ambush.'

'Sundown noticed what they were doing,' Jemima said. 'He's up there, at the cabin.'

'Sundown!' Grey said, his anger rising. 'What happened to Mescal?'

'Come on, Dad,' Jemima said. 'You knew all along who he was, but

193

accepted him and his story out of gratitude, respect for me — '

'He's brought trouble — '

'This land is trouble, and you brought me here — '

'Oh, for God's sake, this is no time — !'

'Damn right it ain't — if you'll pardon me, ma'am,' Jeb Horn said, with obvious chagrin. 'We've got something like an impasse, and family quarrels just waste time. Now, what I suggested still holds good — '

'Only makes carryin' it out a mite trickier,' George Lee said dolefully.

'Hell,' Horn said, 'they'll take one look at you and surrender.'

'You still want us out on the flanks?' said Slim Garratt.

'Yeah, you and Red move out now. Oh, and Slim . . . '

The lanky ranny lifted an eyebrow.

'Keep your eyes skinned. If things ain't workin' out I'll reach up, sweep off my hat.'

The marshal's face was wooden as he

turned to Fleet. 'Ready, Jim?'

'Ready.'

'Grey?'

'We'll be right behind you,' the Englishman said. 'Jemima — you stay put no matter what, you hear?'

With a curt nod, Marshal Jeb Horn drew his rifle and rested it across his thighs, turned his horse and, with George Lee level with him but ten yards out to the side, began the last, dangerous 200 yards into Deacon Wood's Wide Loop.

16

'Too damn quiet.'

They had reached the bluff and started around the shallow curve in the shadows cast by the weakening sun of a winter's afternoon. The two riders were hugging the right bank so that they were tucked under a slight overhang, the branches of the trees above them rattling gently in the dying breeze. Underfoot, a carpet of dead leaves muffled the horses' hoofs.

'What the hell d'you expect?' Jeb Horn said. 'Brass bands and a civic reception?'

Lee chuckled. 'John Grey raised my expectations. Us being officers of the law, and all, appearin' on the scene to show our authority.'

Horn grinned. 'He behind us?'

'Yep. And Slim and Red have gone their separate ways.'

'Red's got it easy. As he works his way around, the bluff'll offer some cover. Slim's way's more open, so . . . '

'So he'll draw their attention,' Lee said bluntly.

'You always were a heartless son of — '

Whatever Horn was about to say was chopped off by the bark of a rifle. It was distant. There was no wicked whine of hot lead. Horn shot Lee a glance as, far away to their left where Slim was closing his arm of the encircling pincers, a pistol snapped in reply.

The sudden shots, distant but startling in the quiet, had disturbed the horses. Horn's mount snorted uneasily and, as George Lee shot a hand forward to fondle suddenly pricked ears, his own horse snorted then blew noisily.

At once, a rifle roared. This time it was close, on top of them. The muzzle flame on top of the bank lit up the shadows. The slug whacked into Lee's saddle-horn to ricochet with a howl and thunk into the dead leaves beneath

Jeb Horn's horse.

Accustomed to moving fast in rattler country, the horse suspected a snake and instantly reared and turned. That move saved Horn. The second shot thrummed through the air where his head had been, a third punched into the horse's head and it went down without a sound.

As the marshal hit the trail in a bruising fall and rolled, George Lee was fighting to control his own spooked mount. Horn saw this, with considerable satisfaction: the shock of the sudden burst of firing was working against the ambushers, and he came to his feet fast under the overhang with his pistol already out and cocked.

He figured one man, no more, and again felt satisfaction at the way things were working out. Wood had slipped up badly. Placing four of his men on the bluff would have stopped the bulk of Circle G dead, left those on the flanks to be mopped up. But Wood had tried to outsmart Horn by spreading his men, and by doing so had created weaknesses.

All those thoughts raced through Horn's mind as he turned to look back the way he had come. He lifted a hand, palm out, to warn Fleet and Grey to stay back, then went up the soft earth at the end of the bluff and into the trees.

A fourth shot blasted, and George Lee roared his fury as he finally lost control, gave his horse its head and clattered down the trail. The gunman threw a fifth shot in that direction. The air was still closing behind the rippling echoes when Horn slipped through the trees towards the overhang and came up behind a man down on one knee with a rifle at his shoulder.

'Enough!' he roared.

Horn's six-gun was up and levelled when the gunman jacked a shell into the breech and spun away from the drop, coming upright with the rifle whipping around. His teeth were bared in a savage grin; were still bared when Horn's shot took him high in the chest, knocked all the breath out of him and sent him backwards off the high bank.

Even as the dead gunman was falling, shooting broke out to the right of the bluff and Horn knew Red had run into trouble. More shots told him Slim was still occupied away over to the left. There was no sight or sound of George Lee.

Then, just as the marshal was working his way through the trees on top of the bluff towards the Wide Loop yard, a fusillade of shots rang out directly ahead and hooves drummed almost beneath him.

He heard Jim Fleet yell, 'Come back, you damn fool,' and glanced down to see John Grey using the ends of his reins to lash his horse along the trail. Seconds later, Fleet came thundering in pursuit.

'Damn, damn, damn!'

Horn broke into a stumbling run over the uneven ground, came out of the trees as the bluff plunged down to the level and the ground melted away to

Wide Loop's yard, saw John Grey already driving on towards the house.

Then, from the barn, a rifle barked, and muzzle flame flashed in a bunkhouse window. Some yards behind Grey, Jim Fleet went tumbling from the saddle to hit the ground like a sack of grain and lie still. John Grey's horse buckled at the knees, went down sliding, and the Englishman was flung clear. Even as he struggled to rise, the gunmen in barn and bunkhouse broke cover and ran towards him.

They were out of pistol range.

But where was George Lee?

Though he ribbed him unmercifully, Horn had enormous respect for his deputy. With Slim and Red fighting on the flanks, Fleet down — maybe dead — and Grey in danger, the short-lived battle was already swinging Deacon Wood's way. He had one man down, but had taken two in return — and, as Horn looked on in dismay, things went from merely bad to complete disaster.

With Jim Fleet down, there was

nobody to hold Jemima Grey — and from back down the trail she had seen her father's horse blasted from under him. Now, hooves drummed as she brought her thoroughbred racing towards Wide Loop. As she did so, John Grey staggered to his feet and began to stumble away from his fallen horse. The gunmen were closing rapidly. He threw a glance over his shoulder, swung towards the bluff and broke into a run.

Inadvertently, he had put himself in the one place he could not be seen by his daughter.

She came on.

From the bluff, Horn roared at her futilely as she thundered by.

Then George Lee appeared, stepping out of nowhere to grab the stumbling rancher, push him out of the way and face the gunmen.

And, as the girl raced across the yard towards her father's fallen horse and the gunmen hesitated, looking from her to George Lee and John

Grey, Deacon Wood appeared on the gallery of the house to grab the battle by the throat.

'Leave them!' he roared. 'Take the girl.'

17

To Billy Sundown, Jemima Grey's departure to warn her father of danger was the moment when truth turned nasty and hit him a cruel blow to the *solar plexus*. He understood well that any man or woman would have made the same decision, but the way she abruptly turned her back on him and in the context of what had gone before and his own musings on what had been and what, considering his actions, was almost certainly to come — he knew that something between them that had not fully started was already finished.

And he realized, with a jolt of surprise, that for this ride from Circle G she had again worn the plaid mackinaw. She was as he had seen her when she had slashed his shoulder-length hair and they rode away from the clearing at Pine Bluffs, and he wondered if this, too, was deliberately done to warn him of her intentions.

So it was with a heavy feeling of emptiness that he watched the girl become a remote, distant rider racing across the grassland towards the group of horsemen, then walked to his horse and prepared to depart. It was from there, in the saddle, that he watched the small Circle G party move towards Wide Loop; from there, turning his horse's head towards the east and his back to the girl who had played such a small but important part in his life, that he heard the first shots and stayed, amazed, to watch the drama unfold.

And when Deacon Wood emerged from the house and stood beneath the tall tree as his two gunmen follow his orders to the letter, Sundown knew that the question he now faced was identical to that posed to Jemima Grey in similar circumstances, and that his answer could be no different.

She could not be abandoned to her fate.

He went about his preparations steadily and without hurry, for he knew that there was now a stand-off in the battle. What he was proposing was a one-man assault on heavily armed men in a position that gave them the advantage. To snatch that advantage from them he needed shock tactics so, with care, he discarded the clothes he had stolen at Pine Bluffs and donned his familiar hip-leggings, breech cloth and moccasins that now smelled strongly of saddle-bag leather.

When he again swung lithely up onto the big dun, the saddle was in Clancy's cabin, his only seat was the blanket damp from the big horse's heat — and he was once more a Cheyenne.

He rode west, again taking a broad sweep, this time to come into Wide Loop from the far side of the corral. As he came down off the ridge the shooting out on both flanks died away. He watched two men ride without concern into the yard and knew that if Slim and Red had fallen, the odds against him had doubled.

Inside him, something primitive stirred.

And in a thin stand of trees to the west of the corral, he sat motionless with the cold air prickling his naked skin and assessed the situation.

From the cabin he had seen one Wide Loop gunman defending the wooded bluff, two out guarding the flanks, two more in barn and bunkhouse and Deacon Wood at the house. Six men. The man on the bluff had taken a slug. The remaining five were holding Jemima.

When the Wide Loop gunman fell, three Circle G men had ridden through after the fourth on the spooked horse. He recognized one, John Grey; the others had to be the lawmen spoken of by Jemima. One of the lawmen, the trail rider, had been shot before they reached the yard. Another had been up on the bluff, on foot, and lagging. John Grey had made it all the way, been downed, but pulled clear by the lawman whose horse had bolted. Out on the flanks, Red and Slim were wounded, or dead.

Circle G were down to three men, and with Jemima in Deacon Wood's hands, they were helpless.

Sundown shifted his weight on the warm blanket, the porcupine quills at his breast whispering like wind-blown twigs. Then he eased the dun forwards and pointed it towards the back of the long, low bunkhouse. At once, he was out in the open, but in no immediate danger: the angle of the buildings meant he could not be seen by any of the Wide Loop men, but was clearly visible from the end of the bluff where Grey and the two lawmen waited.

He was aware of voices, suspected that Grey and the two lawmen were trying to talk sense into Wood from across the yard, then blanked his mind to everything but the task that lay ahead.

Mentally, as he crossed the crisp grass with little more than a wet swishing issuing from beneath the dun's hooves, he was rerunning the series of fleeting, ugly images that had registered as he rode down from the ridge: the gunmen grappling with the struggling Jemima and bundling her away from her father's fallen horse; Wood sadistically twisting her arm up her back as he forced her towards the house while those same two gunmen followed, covering his retreat; the two men who had ridden in from the flanks hastily directed to the abandoned but strategically important positions in the barn and bunkhouse.

Yes, good positions for a man with a rifle facing an adversary he could observe, Sundown admitted, but not so good against an enemy appearing from nowhere with the speed and stealth of a ghost. It would be easy, and quickly finished. The house would be the hard part, with three men guarding the girl. Hard . . . but, again, if he went in fast and the two lawmen were alert to what was happening . . .

The low bunkhouse loomed. He slipped from the dun and flattened himself against the slick logs of the back wall. It was windowless. The only way in was through the door at the front. From there, he could be seen from house and barn. But the door was close to the end of the building. If he moved fast . . .

A thin smile flickered. The odds were already in his favour, but if he was seen, they might improve. Seeing was to become afraid. And fear reduced a man.

Sundown unsheathed his knife.

He went around the end of the bunkhouse like a flicker of light and sprang through the half open door into gloomy warmth. He landed catlike, saw the gunman holding his rifle to one side of the open window, and leaped across the cots even as the man turned, open-mouthed. His shocked squawk was cut off as Sundown grabbed his shirt and pulled him close and a powerful wrist and forearm sank the broad blade to the hilt under his ribs and found the heart. The rifle clattered on the sill. Hot blood gushed over Sundown's fist. He watched the man's eyes glaze, wrenched the knife free with a wet, sucking sound and let him fall soft and heavy to the dirt floor.

He was alone with the silence of the dead.

And now? Go back the way he had come, and circle around to the barn? Or use his appearance to shocking advantage?

He looked at his gory right hand, raised it and daubed his cheeks and forehead with streaks of wet blood that transformed his face into an inhuman mask. The dead man's rifle was balanced on the window sill. Sundown sheathed the knife, took the rifle, jacked a shell into the breech and padded towards the door.

There was no hesitation. A high singing keened in his head, the blood was pulsing in his veins with the beat of a hundred ghostly war drums a matching, soaring echo that propelled him into the light. He sprang through the door and went along the length of the bunkhouse with the rifle barking as he worked the lever and hot lead screamed across the yard to the house where it shattered windows and showered the gallery with glittering shards of glass.

Men began shouting, pistols cracked as they roared their rage, but the shots screamed wild and it was the rage of impotence for the frightened girl they held pinioned could only be used against her father.

Sundown answered the shouts and the shots with a grin of savage joy. He was beyond the bunkhouse, the open door of the barn thirty yards away across open ground. With an ululating howl he sent the rifle spinning and gleaming through the air, then went for the barn at a loping, zigzag run as the gunslingers in the house abandoned six-guns and with more accurate Winchesters kicked the dirt up beneath his skipping, dancing moccasins.

As he ran, the bloody knife leaped into his hand. When he sprang through the open door of the barn, from daylight to shadow, he was met by the dry rustle of straw and the crack of a rifle as the waiting gunslinger frantically backed into the gloom. Sundown felt the tug of a bullet at his hip, a second like an angry hornet stinging his ear. But the gunman was in the grip of a terrible fear. His eyes were wide, his brain transfixed by the sight of the grimacing Indian with the wet red mask and a bloody hand holding high a glittering knife. Even as he watched, horrified, his finger now frozen on the trigger, the arm snapped forward. The knife became a blur. The sound of its whirling flight was an eerie hiss. Then movement and sound ceased with a solid thud. The gunman went down into the straw, the rifle spinning free as both his dying hands grasped the knife jutting from his chest.

And now there was movement in the yard.

In the barn's scented shadows, wiping the knife on the dead man's shirt, Sundown cocked his head at the sounds and experienced a surge of triumph. It took one man to hold the girl, and that man would be Deacon Wood. But if he had sent the two gunmen out after the crazy Cheyenne, he had slipped badly. The yard was open territory, rifle bullets anonymous dealers in death, and this development would bring closer the time when the two lawmen could enter the fight.

But John Grey would not allow them to do that until Jemima was free.

Swiftly, Sundown picked up the dead man's rifle, ran to the back wall of the barn and used the flat of his foot to kick stiff-legged at two loose boards. He ducked through the splintered opening and found himself in long grass and scrub. Thorns ripped at his leggings as he went around the far end of the barn.

He dropped low, peered cautiously

around the end of the wall and saw the house, shattered glass sparkling on the gallery; looked beyond that to the corral and the low, tree-covered bluff away to the right and caught stealthy movement where the three men watched, and waited.

Then closer movement drew his eyes back to the house and he saw a man down on one knee against the wall with a rifle to his shoulder, Quent Yarrow halfway across the yard, rifle at the ready, eyes fixed on the open door of the barn.

Wait!

Yarrow was wary. From the house he had seen the Cheyenne sprint across the yard to the barn, had fallen back in alarm when panes of glass were shockingly blown out of the windows and bullets whined across the room, had listened with savage anger as his cohort's rifle cracked wildly then fell into an ominous silence.

He had already come out second best against the young Cheyenne, and was going nowhere in a hurry. But he was up against an Indian whose whole ethos was patience.

He went forward one slow, hesitant pace, followed it with another, and another. A board creaked as the man on the gallery shifted his weight. Yarrow froze. He glanced back, agitatedly flapped a free hand, turned back to the barn. Went forward. Slowly. A pace at a time. He neared the barn, lifted the rifle — and from thirty yards away Sundown saw him run a tongue over dry lips.

Then he stepped inside, and out of sight.

Sundown lifted the dead man's rifle, stepped out into the open, took careful aim and killed the man on the gallery.

Before the crack of the shot had died, before the man had slumped to the boards, Sundown was away from the barn and racing across the yard. He skirted the big tree, bounded up the steps, sent the rifle spinning end over end. It cracked against the frame then clattered in through the window to the left of the door, and Sundown went across the gallery at an angle and dived in through the window on the other side.

He hit and rolled, already reaching for the knife and, as he came up onto his toes, it seemed that the world slowed down. He heard the rattle of rifle fire and knew that Quent Yarrow had emerged from the barn to be engaged by the lawmen. Across the room, Deacon Wood, with livid weals around his neck and eyes that blazed his hatred, was trying to hold Jemima as she pulled away, then cried out and swung a kick at his groin.

Wood groaned, crumpled, and his hand slipped from her arm. She fell away, flung a terrified glance towards Sundown, pressed white knuckles against her teeth as he watched Deacon Wood fling himself at a gun rack and fumble for a shotgun.

Then again the knife was whispering. It winked in the gloom as it spun across the room, and Deacon Wood went

217

down with his hand touching the Greener but the life that would allow him to use it cut off by the Indian's deadly blade.

Over Wide Loop there fell the silence of death.

★ ★ ★

She was in John Grey's arms.

The two lawmen had come in from the bluff, leading Sundown's horse.

The dead had been tallied, and laid in the barn.

Now, Sundown looked into Grey's eyes, and saw nothing: no hatred, no respect — no thanks.

He looked at the two Dumas lawmen and saw there the intention to do their duty. One, the elder man, even made a move — until John Grey spoke.

'Let him go.'

'He's killed men,' said Jeb Horn.

'If he hadn't, we would have. Indeed,' Grey said, 'you have. But Quent Yarrow would have died anyway for the murder of my foreman . . . ' He shrugged.

'Jim Fleet wanted to take him back to Pine Bluffs.'

'But Fleet's dead,' George Lee said, 'and we ain't got no jurisdiction.'

'Whose side are you on?' Horn said gruffly.

'I just want to go home.'

'Then let him,' John Grey said, and looked at Sundown. 'I hear those savages have moved down to the Red.'

There was silence. In it, Sundown sensed unspoken agreement. He padded across the room and out into the cold air, crunched across the glass-strewn gallery, went down to his horse, then stopped as he heard footsteps.

He turned when she came behind him. As he did, she took the plaid mackinaw and draped it around his shoulders. She did it with gentleness, and the touch of her hands on his shoulders was as magical in its effect as it had been when, mere days ago, she had taken the knife to his hair and begun the work of turning him into a white man.

But her eyes could not leave his face and the drying streaks of blood, and when she averted her head with a shudder she could not disguise he knew that what they had begun was a mistake, and there was nothing for him here.

He swung himself lithely up onto the dun. He sensed her presence on the gallery, knew she had again turned and that her blue eyes were watching him. Then, without a word, Billy Sundown dug in his heels, rode fast out of the Wide Loop yard and pointed the dun's nose towards the distant Red River.

THE END

We do hope that you have enjoyed reading this large print book.

Did you know that all of our titles are available for purchase?

We publish a wide range of high quality large print books including:
Romances, Mysteries, Classics
General Fiction
Non Fiction and Westerns

Special interest titles available in large print are:
The Little Oxford Dictionary
Music Book, Song Book
Hymn Book, Service Book

Also available from us courtesy of Oxford University Press:
Young Readers' Dictionary
(large print edition)
Young Readers' Thesaurus
(large print edition)

For further information or a free brochure, please contact us at:
Ulverscroft Large Print Books Ltd.,
The Green, Bradgate Road, Anstey,
Leicester, LE7 7FU, England.
Tel: (00 44) **0116 236 4325**
Fax: (00 44) **0116 234 0205**

THE CHISELLER

Tex Larrigan

Soon the paddle steamer would be on its long journey down the Missouri River to St Louis. Now, all Saul Rhymer had to do was to play the last master stroke of the evening. He looked at the mounting pile of gold and dollar bills and again at the cards in his hand. Then, looking around the table, he produced the deed to the goldmine in Montana. 'Let's play poker!' But little did he know how that journey back to St Louis would change his life so drastically.

THE ARIZONA KID

Andrew McBride

When former hired gun Calvin Taylor took the job of sheriff of Oxford County, New Mexico, it was for one reason only — to catch, or kill, the notorious Arizona Kid, and pick up the fifteen hundred dollars reward the governor had secretly offered. Taylor found himself on the trail of the infamous gang known as the Regulators, hunting down a man who'd once been his friend. The pursuit became, in every sense, a journey of death.

BULLETS IN BUZZARDS CREEK

Bret Rey

The discovery of a dead saloon girl is only the beginning of Sheriff Jeff Gilpin's problems. Fortunately, his old friend 'Doc' Holliday arrives in Buzzards Creek just as Gilpin is faced by an outlaw gang. In a dramatic shoot-out the sheriff kills their leader and Holliday's reputation scares the hell out of the others. But it isn't long before the outlaws return, when they know Holliday is not around, and Gilpin is alone against six men . . .

THE YANKEE HANGMAN

Cole Rickard

Dan Tate was given a virtually impossible task: to save the murderer Jack Williams from the condemned cell. Williams, scum that he was, held a secret that was dear to the Confederate cause. But if saving Williams would test all Dan's ingenuity, then his further mission called for immense courage and daring. His life was truly on the line and if he didn't succeed, Horace Honeywell, the Yankee Hangman would have the last word!

MISSOURI PALACE

S. J. Rodgers

When ex-lawman Jim Williams accepts the post of security officer on the *Missouri Palace* riverboat, he finds himself embroiled in a power struggle between Captain J. D. Harris and Jake Farrell, the murderous boss of Willow Flats, who will stop at nothing to add the giant sidepaddler to his fleet. Williams knows that with no one to back him up in a straight fight with Farrell's hired killers, he must hit them first and hit them hard to get out alive.